Still With You

BAXTER BOYS
BOOK THREE

JESSIE GUSSMAN

Contents

Acknowledgments   v

Chapter 1   1
Chapter 2   9
Chapter 3   18
Chapter 4   30
Chapter 5   38
Chapter 6   47
Chapter 7   53
Chapter 8   60
Chapter 9   66
Chapter 10   82
Chapter 11   84
Chapter 12   93
Chapter 13   102
Chapter 14   110
Chapter 15   119
Chapter 16   129
Chapter 17   136
Chapter 18   143
Chapter 19   152
Epilogue   159

Sneak Peek of Second Chance With You   163
Read More Jessie!   167
A Gift from Jessie   169
Escape to more faith-filled romance series by Jessie Gussman!   171

Acknowledgments

Cover art by Julia Gussman
Editing by Heather Hayden
Narration by Jay Dyess
Author Services by CE Author Assistant

~

Listen to the unabridged audio for FREE performed by Jay Dyess on the Say with Jay channel on YouTube. Get early access to all of Jay's recordings and listen to Jessie's books before they're available to the general public, plus get daily Bible readings by Jay and bonus scenes by becoming a Say with Jay channel member.

To Miss Betty, Miss Angelina and Miss Alda

When my children were little, we were asked to sing on a regular basis at a local assisted living facility and nursing home. I had no idea why anyone would want to hear our family sing, but when God opens a door, I try to walk through.

We had so much fun over the years—you haven't lived until you've participated in wheelchair square dancing!!—and met so many wonderful people. Mostly ladies.

One woman, as she grew older, lost the ability to speak in any language except the German of her childhood. I still remember her singing in her native tongue, tears streaming down her face. The tune was easily recognizable as Amazing Grace—haunting and beautiful in any language. She made my kids cry and they didn't even know why.

But the ladies that stand out to me the most were the ones with perpetual positive attitudes and constant smiles. We were there to entertain them, but they cheered this young mother by how they faced their many trials with courage and joy.

Their unbending faith, their words of wisdom, their unconditional love for my children, and their constant support and encouragement were a source of inspiration to me.

Those days are past. My children are grown, and the ladies are gone now. However, I'll always have the memories that serve as a guide to the woman I have yet to become.

Miss Alda, Miss Betty and Miss Angelina, I want to be just like you when I grow up.

Chapter One

Harris Winsted opened the heavy library door, shifted the massive bulk of papers and books in her arms, and stepped out into the brisk evening air. It had cost her a modest fortune, which was no insignificant thing on her small-town librarian's salary, but she had printed off the copyright-allotted thirty copies of the production of *Annie* the community players were doing to raise money for a children's library at the new pediatric cancer hospital.

Two opposing pangs pushed through her chest. Excitement and fear. Being able to sponsor a library for kids in the hospital was a dream come true for her. After all, she knew exactly how it felt to be cooped up for months on end having read everything in sight, including every word on the shampoo bottles, at least five times. But she'd never directed a play before in her life. At least she wasn't acting in it. Getting up in front of people was a phobia she'd never conquered.

After juggling her keys and locking the door, she started down the small flight of steps that led to the sidewalk. A man's shout broke the stillness of the early fall air. A child's higher-pitched yell followed, then what sounded like a war-hoot from an elderly man. Harris smiled. It sounded like a family was having fun down the side alley that ran along the library. The next best thing to a family reading together was a family playing together.

She shoved down the tiny thread of longing that surged in her chest. The cancer treatments she'd had as a child had wiped any hope of having her own children from her life. She was too studious and serious to have children of her own anyway.

The stomping of footsteps declared they were now running. It almost sounded like the whirl of a bike tire back there too.

Her high heel clicked on the cement as she stepped off the last step onto the sidewalk. The laughing and shouting had gotten closer. She shifted the heavy stack of papers, wishing that the hole punch hadn't chosen today to get stuck in the closed position. No amount of grunting, pushing, or under-her-breath—because it was a library after all—swearing had managed to get it to work. So her precious, expensive copies of *Annie* lay stacked, alternated by long and short edge, on top of the pile of books she was delivering to the assisted care facility on her way home.

The shouts got louder as a blur from her left made her turn her head. Barely able to see over the top of her pile of books and precious papers, she blinked. Then squinted. It wasn't every day one saw a wheelchair rounding the corner on two wheels. She looked just as the man in it was smiling so hard his teeth popped out. They fell to the cement as the much younger man pushing it cornered sharply, the chair almost horizontal to the ground. The man's biceps bulged. A helmeted boy on rollerblades, legs churning, screamed, "I'm going to win! You can't beat me!" as his right skate hit the dentures. His hands windmilled, florescent green sleeves a blur as his shouted challenge turned to a startled yelp. The dentures skidded to the side where one of the younger man's scuffed brown boots nicked them, throwing him off balance. Harris's eyebrows flew up to her hairline. Her brain shouted at her feet to pedal backward, but in the heels, they were slow to respond.

The boy grabbed the wheelchair handle to keep from falling. Able to right the chair despite the added pressure, the man pushing the chair overcompensated, and he took two wild, uncoordinated steps before his body crashed into Harris.

Papers and books flew everywhere.

As she flew downward toward the ground, she couldn't help but try to search her memory...were the pages numbered?

Fully expecting to crack her head on the cement steps, Harris was surprised to land with a thump on the solid chest of the pusher.

She had no idea how he'd managed to reverse their positions before they hit the ground, but she was grateful, except...

The man's ball cap had gone askew, and his curling brown hair and laughing brown eyes were now visible. Turbo Baxter.

Harris felt her cheeks heat and knew her entire face would be as red as her hair. All seven million of her freckles would be camouflaged under that brighter color. Unfortunately, her complexion looked even worse as fire-engine red than it did as the regular porcelain white splotched with enough freckles to cover the north side of the Empire State Building. Twice.

"I should have known when I heard that unholy screeching that you had something to do with it," she said to the man under her. She blew a hair out of her eyes and tried to figure out how she was going to get off him since she'd foolishly decided to wear a pencil skirt and skyscraper heels today.

She couldn't look at Turbo again. With amusement crinkling his eyes, and with his sharp Roman nose and angled jaw, the man was sinfully handsome—cover model material for the romance novels she loved to read at night—but he had the maturity level of a two-year-old. She wouldn't be horizontal with her papers scattered to the four winds if he had the sense God gave a squirrel.

He grunted under her. "I should have known that you'd manage to turn a simple footrace into an obstacle course." His biceps flexed, stretching the sleeves of his t-shirt as he shifted, pushing her off and up, away from the intriguing scent of raw masculinity overlaid with just a hint of fun. A scent she remembered clearly from last summer's wedding when she had the misfortune to be in the same bridal party as Turbo. She had been lucky enough to have not seen him since.

"I'm sorry my presence on the sidewalk confused you." She brushed her skirt off and looked at the boy, who didn't seem to be bleeding, then at the old man in the wheelchair who had somehow gotten his dentures off the ground and was using his shirt to wipe them off. He popped them into his mouth before holding out his hand in a somehow gallant gesture.

"That's Mr. Pollack. But everyone calls him Pap," Turbo said from above her shoulder. "Pap, this is the fussy librarian, Ms. Winsted." Turbo ducked down and started picking up papers.

Harris cringed at his calloused unconcern for her precious play copies and narrowed her eyes, but she didn't get a chance to say anything before Pap spoke. "I'm so sorry Turbo ran into you. Typically, he runs away from women."

"I think you have that backward," Harris muttered as she shook his hand.

"DeShaun, help Turbo gather the nice lady's papers up, please," the elderly man said, waving a gnarled hand around. Her papers littered the ground like a blanket. At least it wasn't windy.

"I wouldn't say 'nice,'" Turbo mumbled under his breath. "Prissy, maybe."

"I can hear you," Harris spat out at him as she bent and picked up several papers. They weren't numbered. Just her luck.

"I'm sorry."

Her hand, holding a fistful of papers, stilled. She turned slowly. Turbo Baxter had just apologized. His face actually oozed sincerity.

"I shouldn't have gotten so upset about you deliberately stepping right in front of us, on purpose. Then you shoved me down and fell on top of me, and you're not exactly a lightweight." Turbo lifted his hat and shoved a hand through his longish curls. His lip twitched, ruining the earnestness of his apology as if his words already hadn't.

Harris's lips compressed together. That's exactly what Turbo had done at the wedding last year when she'd been stuck in the bridal party with him, and it's exactly what he'd done in high school. Not that she'd spent much time with him then, either. Although her most unforgettable high school memory had to be when she'd been voted most studious and he'd been voted class clown. They had to get their picture taken together. The photographer thought it would be funny to snap a pic of Harris reading a book with Turbo on a chair behind her pretending to be about to pour red paint over her head. Apparently, among his other numerous faults, Turbo didn't know what pretending meant, since he dumped the entire one-gallon can of fire-engine red paint on her. It made for a great picture, she supposed. But he ruined her dogeared version of *Anne of Green Gables*, which she had lovingly chosen from her numerous, beloved favorites to be the book in the photo. Then he spent the rest of the year making fun of her that he'd actually found something that was redder than her hair.

That might have been ten years ago, and she might have spent the last decade avoiding him, despite living in the same small town.

Keeping her back to him, she continued to pick her papers up. She'd learned in high school that the best way to deal with Turbo was to ignore him.

"Hey." He grabbed her elbow. "You're actually bleeding here. And I really am sorry."

She yanked her arm away and continued to pick up papers. The little boy chattered, handing his papers to the old man who tapped the piles against his leg and straightened them out a little before stacking them on his knees.

Harris's chest tightened. Hopefully she'd be able to put these scripts back together. She moved away from Turbo. He was probably just going to tell her he was joking, or she'd look up and he'd squirt ketchup on her or something equally annoying. Although her elbow did hurt. Like a brush burn. She'd look at it later.

Turbo appeared in her peripheral vision, knees bent, picking up papers and shuffling them together haphazardly. She turned from him and moved away before she said something really nasty.

He moved with her. "I'm serious. I didn't mean to run into you."

She didn't look at him. "Okay. So you're admitting it was your fault."

"And I'm apologizing. The nice thing is to say 'hey, it's okay.'"

"Well, it's really not okay. I just paid a fortune to buy the copyright to thirty scripts and print them off, and now they're all mixed up and practically ruined."

"I wish I could fix it. I really am sorry."

"Stop saying you're sorry!" She brushed her hair back over her shoulder. Her gaze fixed on a shiny, bright red drop on the paper she'd been about to pick up. Looked like blood. Great.

"I don't know how else to get you to believe me." He picked up the paper with the blood, looking at her. His nearness was distracting, and she went back to swiping papers from the sidewalk in order to keep from meeting his gaze.

The little boy had gathered all her books and straightened up after stacking them in a pile on the library steps.

She scooted away from Turbo, holding tight to her irritation. "If you're really sorry, you can help me arrange these papers in order and put them all back together." It would take hours. All night possibly. And she had wanted to hand out the scripts tomorrow evening at the first rehearsal. She held tight to a fistful of papers and stopped long enough to see Turbo's reaction.

He sighed and looked down at the papers. "Aren't they numbered?"

"No." She set her jaw against his crestfallen look.

His Adam's apple bobbed, and a muscle twitched in his jaw. "Oh." He turned away, bending over and grabbing the last few papers off the sidewalk. He shuffled them into a pile, reached down, and took the papers Pap handed him, awkwardly smoothing them altogether. "Here."

"You're not helping?" She didn't really want him to; he'd find a way to set her house on fire or defrost all the food in her freezer or paint her car pink or...something. After all, it was Turbo. But it was his fault that she had all the scattered papers to begin with. Although...

She looked at Pap, sitting in his chair while the little boy showed him something on his phone. Really, she needed to give Turbo points for hanging out with an elderly man and a young kid. It was Friday evening. He could be at a bar, trying to find a date for the night.

"No. I..." Turbo glanced at the man and boy. "I have plans for this evening."

Pap looked up from his chair. "Humph. Your only plans for this evening involved taking me back to prison, ahem, the nursing joint my daughters dumped me in then never visit, and flirting with Mrs. Silcrest while we play bingo. And trust me, Sally Silcrest will miss you, but your so-called 'stuffy librarian' is much better looking, not to mention about seventy years younger."

"Sally was going to bake me cookies," Turbo said. He shifted and shoved a hand in his front pocket. "Nothing's better than Sally's fresh-baked chocolate chips."

"Of course, Mr. Baxter." It hurt more than she cared to admit that he'd rather spend the evening at the nursing home watching the elderly residents play bingo than have to be in her presence for a few hours. But he probably did liven up the old folks' home. Wherever Turbo was, people were laughing. "I wouldn't want you to miss cookies, bingo, and flirting with a 90-year-old. I'll organize my own papers."

Harris put her nose in the air to hide her hurt and turned, bending to pick up the stack of books. Blood dripped from her arm to the step.

"She's bleeding all over the place," Pap said.

"Wow. She definitely needs a couple band-aids." The little boy scrunched up his face. "That's nasty."

"You're right, DeShaun." Turbo reached into his back pocket and pulled out a blue rag. "Let me see that." He reached for her elbow.

She would bleed out before she let him touch her with that dirty rag. Whether he used it to wipe his hands after working on his truck or to wipe his nose, the rag looked well-worn. "No thank you." She tried not to sound stuck-up, but she wasn't going to risk contracting flesh-eating bacteria by being polite in this instance. "I'll be fine until I get home."

"But..." DeShaun said.

Turbo's hands paused midair, and she was pretty sure he was offended.

"I'll be fine. Really." She tried to speak in a kind tone but to still be very firm. That rag was not touching her arm. She forced more words out. "Thanks for helping me clean up my papers." Even if it had been his fault they were dropped in the first place.

Guilt squeezed her throat. She'd known the hole punch was on its last legs. She should have replaced it before it quit.

Her arm burned.

"I can carry those books for you," Turbo said in a low tone as she started to walk away. "You taking them to your car?"

"No. To Redbud Manor."

"That's where we're going," DeShaun sang out. "Come on, Pap.

We'll beat the slowpokes." He pushed the wheelchair down the sidewalk, gliding behind on his rollerblades.

Harris tightened her lips. If only she had known. She would have said she was going in the opposite direction, just to get away from Turbo. Too late. Although, if she had to walk in the same direction as him, she might as well let him carry the books. Not the papers.

She turned back around to see him watching her. Turbo with those brown eyes hooded under his ball cap. Probably his next prank was simmering in his brain, and she'd be on the receiving end. Well, he could still carry the books.

As soon as she looked at him, he stepped forward with his hands out, reaching for her books. Against her better judgment, she held them out, trying to separate them from the stack of papers under them. How could she not notice his hands which were strong and tanned with long fingers? Capable hands. Hands that knew how to work. Hands that could grip an old man's wheelchair and race down the street, making the fellow laugh while racing with a young boy who seemed to be having a great time. His fingers curled around her books, and a surprising bit of heat curled in her stomach.

One of the books started to slide, and they both reached for it. Their hands clashed together. Shockwaves rolled up her arm, intensifying the burning in her elbow. Her startled gaze flew to his. Close enough now that she could see his eyes under the curled brim of his cap, she watched as they widened as though mirroring her own.

She searched his face, noticed the tightening of his jaw, the small twitch of his lips, before feeling the shifting pile of books and grabbing for them. Turbo's hands reached out at the same time, and they collided again, only this time she lost her grip on everything, and it all fell down again. Papers and books back in a heaped-up mess on the sidewalk.

Chapter Two

Turbo cursed his stupid clumsiness. Normally he was surehanded as well as surefooted, but Harris had the ability to bring out the very worst in him. Always had. From that time in high school when he'd accidentally dropped that entire can of red paint over her, to the time he'd toilet papered her house thinking it belonged to the chemistry teacher who'd given him an F, despite the extra credit he'd paid the valedictorian to do for him.

And of course, he'd had to joke about it. It was his default way of dealing with life. He'd been doing better lately, but again, Harris brought out the worst in him.

His mouth moved before he could stop it. "You did that on purpose just so you could see me on my hands and knees at your feet again, didn't you?"

Harris's mouth opened and closed, and he cursed his flapping tongue. It had been obvious the last time that her papers were uber-important. He should have been more careful. And he shouldn't have joked about it this time. Harris never did think his jokes were funny. He'd had the biggest crush on her in high school. But the more he tried to make her laugh, the more annoyed she got at him. He'd finally given up. On making her laugh, anyway. The crush hadn't gone away quite as easily. Kinda felt like it was still there, actually.

His eyes skimmed over the adorable freckles on her face, avoiding her glare, before he knelt at her feet. "Oh, Queen Harris, I pay thee homage..."

"Shut up, Turbo."

He started to gather up her papers, which hadn't scattered quite so badly this time. "I thought you liked Shakespeare."

"That wasn't Shakespeare."

"It was pretty darn close. Give me a few more minutes, and I'll think of something that rhymes with Harris and really wow you."

"That's not going to happen."

"What? Me wowing you? Of course it is."

"You thinking," she snapped, grabbing her papers with more force this time. She wasn't even trying to keep from wrinkling them.

"Whatever." He snatched up the last ones and straightened. "Here, I already have it. Oh, Queen Harris. I hope I don't embarrass, you in Paris, with hair like carrots."

If it were possible, she jerked to a stop, and her gaze drilled holes in his skull. "What. Did. You. Say?" she said through clenched teeth.

"You liked it, didn't you?" He grinned. He hadn't done anything offensive, nothing that involved paint or toilet paper anyway, so she had to be faking her anger. She'd be smiling any minute.

"You said my hair was like carrots."

"Carrots kind of rhymed."

"Have you ever read *Anne of Green Gables*?"

"Nope," he said easily. He didn't have to think about it. He'd never actually read a book.

She rolled her eyes. "Of course."

The thought finally hit him that she wasn't going to laugh. And then he remembered why he avoided books, libraries, and, most of all, librarians. Everything, every single thing, that they did reminded them of some ridiculous book reference. It was like they spoke in code most of the time. After all, when one didn't read books, one hardly got the book jokes.

Harris had always had that mysterious way about her. Still, he'd crushed on her big time, not just because he found her green eyes, auburn hair, and light, almost translucent skin with the overlay of freckles fascinating, but because when she didn't have her nose in a book, she was quietly seeking out and talking to the kids that seemed left out and alone. He'd seen her helping kids like himself with homework and reading assignments. Never him. But kids like him. The ones the teachers didn't want to bother with because they'd already been labeled as stupid or slow.

It bothered him. Mostly because it was true. He was stupid. He was slow. And he couldn't read. Which was why he avoided libraries and librarians. And it was why he'd told Harris no, he couldn't help her put her papers back together. Without numbers, how the heck would he figure out which paper went where?

"Are you done insulting me?" Harris asked. One hip jutted out, but she had both hands in a death grip on the stack of papers.

"Are you done making ridiculous accusations?" he asked. When had he insulted her? He bent and scooped up her stack of books. "Come on, we'd better catch up to Pap and DeShaun. Pap can handle himself, but I signed him out of the home, so if anything happens to him, his daughters will be down my throat."

She sighed and fell into step beside him; from the droop of her shoulders, she'd resigned to walk with him. Funny, no matter how hard he tried, he'd never been able to impress her. Guess some things never changed. He'd thought his little rhyme was pretty funny and kind of good for being spur of the moment.

He shrugged it off. Probably was too much of a stretch for the serious librarian to be interested in the brainless truck driver who couldn't even read.

Harris's phone rang.

He shoved the books into one arm and held his other out for the papers. "I'll take them," he said.

"No." The word came out clipped, like she was angry, and he wondered what he'd done this time. Or maybe she was still mad from last time, whatever he'd done. She clutched the papers to her chest as she fumbled in her purse, one handed, for her phone.

She finally got it, swiping and holding it to her ear. "Hello?"

Turbo kicked a small rock off the sidewalk, listening unashamed to her conversation.

Harris gasped. "No!" A pause. "I mean, I'm happy for you. Thrilled... Yes, I know this is the opportunity of a lifetime. No, really. I'll be fine... Sure, of course. Call your family. They're going to be so excited for you... Thanks. I'd love tickets. Great... Bye."

Her rigid posture slumped as her hand dropped to her side. She closed her eyes for a second and sighed.

"Hey, watch where you're going." Turbo grabbed her arm as she almost tripped over a weed-covered crack in the sidewalk.

"Thanks." Her voice was soft and subdued.

"Someone killed your pet kitten?"

One lip pulled back, and she gave him a look.

"No? Worse?" He pretended to think. "Your mother's stuck in jail in Iran and won't make your birthday party."

She gave a little snort. "That might actually be a good thing, but no."

A good thing? Interesting. "So, what could be worse than dead kittens and mothers in jail? Hmm." He glanced sideways at her. Still no smile, but her face didn't look quite as pinched. "The Russians developed a bug that destroys coffee beans, and in ten days, the world's supply of coffee will be exhausted."

One corner of her mouth turned up. "Maybe if that were cocoa beans and chocolate..."

"So that's it? That's what has you so bummed? Chocolate shortage?" He shook his head. "Man, some people are so shallow."

She did laugh that time, and he felt a thrill of victory shoot up his chest.

"Hey. It's not shallow. Millions of people are dependent on the chocolate trade for their livelihood." Her face fell, and Turbo was suddenly aware of dusk falling. "That's not it. I'm raising money to buy books for the library in the new pediatric hospital that just opened by staging a production of *Annie*." She lifted her arms a fraction, indicating the papers in them. "My leading man just got offered a role on an off-Broadway production. He has to back out. We were supposed to start practicing tomorrow." She threw her head back and exhaled sharply. "My scripts are a jumbled mess, I have no leading man, and if it weren't so important for those kids to have access to books, I'd..."

"Go hide in your closet and hoard chocolate bars?" Turbo suggested.

"That actually sounds like a good idea right now." Harris didn't smile.

As they rounded the corner, Pap and DeShaun came into sight, waiting at the entrance to the assisted care facility.

"If you really want to help me, you could use the activity room tables to start sorting these scripts." Harris nodded at the haphazard bunch of papers in her arms.

Uh...

He was saved from answering by DeShaun. "Losers! You're not even running," he scoffed, little boy fashion.

"You get a little older, son, and you'll slow down for a pretty girl too." Pap smacked the top of DeShaun's helmet.

"Girls are dumb." DeShaun wrapped both arms around Pap and squeezed. "I'm going home." He straightened and looked at Turbo. "You still coming later?"

Turbo nodded. "You get your homework done, and I'll be there to whoop your butt on *Space Lizards* at least once."

"Ah, man, it's Friday night. I don't have to have my homework done until Sunday."

"That's right. But I'm not playing *Space Lizards* if it's not done when I stop in."

"That sucks. But you're the only one that can get through the Alligator Belt." DeShaun kicked the sidewalk, making his rollerblades spin.

"I'll bring Mrs. Silcrest's cookies, too."

"Hope they're the ones with the icing."

"She knows you like 'em. Take a shower, and I'll make sure Mrs. Silcrest's cookies have icing."

DeShaun snorted. "That's because you'll flirt with her and she'll do anything you want. She thinks you're *hand-some*." His voice went high and singsong on the last word.

Turbo held out a fist to bump then did the short hand motions he and DeShaun had made up as their own special handshake.

"That's because I am, you little turkey."

"Quit calling me a turkey, dork." DeShaun gave his hand a final slap before skating off.

"He lives close?" Harris asked with a wrinkled brow and a concerned look at the darkening sky.

"Yeah."

"It's not far from the library. Wonder why I've never seen him there?"

Turbo stared at her from under his ball cap. She sounded truly puzzled, like a kid would voluntarily go to the library if there was anything else they could be doing instead. He'd rather scrub out garbage cans, put a roof on in one-hundred-degree weather, or paint high-powered electrical lines wrapped in tinfoil.

Had he ever set foot in a library without being forced? Stupid question because the answer was an obvious no. Harris seemed serious, though.

He shrugged. "Maybe he's allergic to bookworms. Are they gluten free?"

Harris narrowed her eyes. "Maybe he hangs around with people who would rather play video games than read."

Turbo looked away. "Yeah. That must be it."

Pap had made it to the door. They opened it, and he wheeled in. He'd be in a big rush to catch the tail end of supper and be able to regale all the other residents about their adventures this afternoon before bingo started in a half an hour. Before rounding the corner headed toward his room, Pap looked back at them and smirked, lifting his fingers in a little wave. Turbo could almost imagine he was going to gleefully inform Mrs. Silcrest that her cookies had lost out to another woman's red hair and books. If only.

"So, Pap is your dad, and DeShaun is your son?" Harris asked in a distracted tone as she set the papers down on an empty counter and started to go through them, flipping them over so they were all facing up. He could do that.

He set the books down and took the papers. "Deliver your books.

I've got this." She glanced over at him with one brow raised, reminding him he'd not answered her question.

He met her eyes. "No and no."

"Shouldn't you be out with some hot date soaking up the neon lights? It's Friday night after all," she said as she focused on sorting through the pile of books.

"Is that what you think I should be doing?" he asked in a low tone, trying to copy her disinterested air.

She shrugged, studying the spine of a book before placing it in a pile of its own.

His chest pinched, and his mouth started running to cover it. "It's Friday, and you're obviously not going on a hot date either. Is this your way of begging me for a date? Because you already heard, I've got bingo and a sweet lady who's making me cookies. With icing. Then I've got a video game championship to win, and that could take all night. So, as fun as it would be to spout poetry and buy flowers, I'm booked."

She started sputtering halfway through his speech and barely waited for him to stop before she shrilled, "I wasn't begging for a date."

He shrugged, keeping his head down and pretending to be absorbed in fixing the papers so she wouldn't see his grin. "You have your version, I have mine."

"Yours is the made-up fantasy version."

"Seems fitting, since you live in a fantasy world." He jerked a thumb at her books. "It's okay though, 'cause I can cancel my plans to get drunk and find a hot chick tomorrow night and take you out. Although there won't be poetry."

"I'm busy," Harris bit out.

"I'm not." The perky, blond nurse that was often on evening shift walked up behind them. "If you're offering dates, I'll take you up on it." She laughed and grabbed his arm, looking up and winking. "I can be just as much fun as you."

"I bet you can." He looked at her nametag. It started with a "T," but he couldn't remember, so he winked instead. He managed to keep from backpedaling only by imagining Harris laughing at him as he struggled to get away from the clinging hand. "I was kidding, though. I'm definitely busy tomorrow night."

"I heard you were getting drunk and picking up hot chicks. I can help with that."

Harris snorted softly.

"Um, actually, no. I, uh, I've got something else, I..." He cleared his throat. "I have to work on my truck." He shifted away, and her arm dropped. He bent his head over the papers like he was doing something that needed a lot of concentration.

"I can help."

He flashed his dimples at her before looking back down. "I'll let you know if I need any."

"Text me."

"Sure thing." If he had her number. Which he didn't.

T-nurse walked off. Turbo glanced at Harris. She'd finished sorting her books and had two in each hand.

"When you're done there, just let the pile sit unless you want to start working on getting thirty scripts separated and in order. I need to deliver the books."

He'd kind of expected Harris to tease him about T-nurse, but it was Harris, and she had her serious face back on. Did she ever let loose and smile, laugh with abandon? Man, he wanted to find out. No, he wanted to be the one to make her laugh.

He fixed the last paper in the pile and set the stack down. "I've got time; I can deliver the books."

"That's great." She dug through her purse for a pen and a sheet of paper. "Here are the names of the residents I visit. Just write down the names of the titles they want to borrow for next week, and cross off the names of the books they give you back."

Heavy and hot, Turbo's stomach dropped while his chest tightened and squeezed. "Uh..." He was an expert at getting out of situations where he had to read or write. Sure, he could recognize his name and a few easy words, but there was no way he could do what she'd just asked.

He glanced down at the paper and pen she held out to him then to the stack of books. His face flushed hot then cold.

He forced his lips to quirk in a devious grin and lifted a brow. Taking the paper from her hand, he said, "I bet you have this list all organized and easy to follow."

Her face revealed no hint of distress.

He nodded, pretending to try to hide his smirk. "I think this could be fun."

Her brows drew down.

"Yeah." He glanced at the first room number on the list then grabbed a stack of two books from the middle of the line Harris had organized. "I think the resident in room 203 would like these books more than the ones she asked for."

Yep. She opened her mouth to protest. He flashed his best cocky grin and turned.

"No. Wait." Harris stomped her foot. "Forget it. I can tell you're going to screw everything up, probably on purpose. I'll just do it myself."

"Nah. Don't worry about it. They'll thank me eventually. I'm going to broaden their reading tastes."

She snatched the paper out of his hand and held her hand out for the books. "Hand them over."

He acted reluctant, trying to look guilty and innocent at the same time. Meanwhile, his heart beat painfully, and the back of his throat tightened. What would it be like to actually be real? He shoved that thought down as soon as it appeared. Harris would hate him more than she already did if she knew the truth.

Chapter Three

"'An elephant's faithful, one hundred percent.'" Harris finished *Horton Hatches the Egg* and closed the book. The children at her feet groaned and begged for another story until the teenaged helper at the afterschool activity center gathered them up and shuffled them over to the gym floor for game time.

Gathering up the other books that she'd brought from the library to read, Harris stood and walked over to the kitchenette area where her friends, Cassidy and Kelly, stood chatting while Cassidy's two-year-old twins toddled around with their sippy cups.

Monday and Thursday evenings after the library closed, Harris always tried to come and read a few books to the kids at the center. She loved helping the kids, and sometimes it was the only time she got to see Cassidy and Kelly, now that they were both married. To Turbo's brothers.

"That's one of my favorite books," Kelly said as Harris set the pile down with Horton on top.

"Me too." Which was why she brought it so often. She slumped down on a barstool but tried to put a smile on her face. "How is everything going with both of you?"

"Life is still crazy and doesn't seem like it's going to get any calmer any time soon," Cassidy said with a laugh.

"Not until the kids turn eighteen and leave for college," Harris said, referring to the three kids that Cassidy and Torque had adopted.

"How's your play coming?" Kelly asked, pushing aside her clipboard and taking the empty sippy cup one of the twins handed her.

"It's not," Harris said.

"What?" Kelly and Cassidy froze, staring at Harris.

Cassidy took Harris's hand across the countertop. "You've been setting this up for months. You've gotten permission to use the theater, the hospital is planning on you—they even made you your own room."

"I'm just going to have to find something else to do to raise money. Daddy Warbucks got an off-Broadway offer, and I don't blame him for not turning it down."

"Camila was thrilled about playing Annie. Have you told her?" Kelly finished filling the sippy cup up and handed it back to the twin.

"No. I cancelled last week's practices, but I just couldn't cancel the whole play. I spent the weekend trying to figure out who could play Daddy Warbucks, I even called a few people..."

Kelly and Cassidy exchanged a look. Both of them knew that Harris hated talking on the phone. So it was a pretty big deal that she'd not only made personal calls, but that she'd been asking for a favor.

"It's no use. Everyone is too busy or not interested. I don't blame them for not wanting to get up in front of people. Directing and producing it was more than I could handle anyway. I'm such a dreamer sometimes." Her back slumped, and she had to refrain from putting her head down on the counter.

"Well, I'd do it for you if I could." Kelly slipped over and took Harris's other hand.

"Me too. I could do Daddy Warbucks easily, but you might get tired of all my kids running around the practice." Cassidy grinned and picked up the twin that was whining at her feet. Nissa, Harris thought. They were hard to tell apart.

"Yeah, I know you guys would help me if you could. You just can't be men, and right now I need a man." She grinned a little as she said it, and Turbo's face popped into her mind.

She'd been thinking about him a lot since they spent Friday evening at the nursing home. She'd always thought he was a big flirt, and he did flirt shamelessly with the ladies in the home, but he'd almost seemed like he wanted to run from the flirty nurse, who was his age and let him know loud and clear that she was available. Harris had found it kind of funny to see him shifting and uncomfortable, but she wasn't sure she would have noticed if Pap hadn't said that Turbo usually ran from women, not into them. After she'd thought about it—and she had to admit she'd thought about that almost as much as she'd thought about what to do about her play production—she'd realized that Turbo was happy-go-lucky and always surrounded by girls and boys in high school, but he'd never been with just one girl. Not that she knew of. Not that she'd kept track of him over the last decade or so.

"I'd even say I'd try to get Tough to do it, but our marriage is kind of new to be straining it in that way. Not to mention, he's not exactly the kind of guy who loves attention. I think you can relate." Kelly gave Harris a knowing look. Harris had to nod. She, herself, had no desire to get on that stage. But they had all the female parts covered.

"Torque might." Cassidy gave her daughter a kiss and set her back down on the floor. "I know he wouldn't want to, but he might do it to help the kids."

"I could probably get enough donations to get the library started without the money from the play if I pounded the pavement and hit up all the normal donors, but I really wanted to raise awareness of it in the community, to get the community behind it, and a play would do it." Harris dropped her chin in her hand. "Do you really think Torque might play the part?"

Cassidy smiled, but it wasn't filled with confidence. "I'll try."

TURBO DOWNSHIFTED, feeling the smooth bump as the cogs caught. He depressed the accelerator, the RPMs hiked, and all five hundred horses hit the ground, pulling. The combination of power and torque vibrated through the steering wheel as his rig pulled the steep mountain road on State Route 22. He grinned. The old girl was pulling her guts out.

Checking the temperature, he flipped the fan on manual, feeling the rig slow even more as it pulled power from the engine to run the big blades.

As much as he'd love to admire the crisp blue sky and orange-frosted green leaves, the mill in Gettysburg was out of corn and needed the twenty-eight ton he had in his belt trailer in order to resume production.

"Come on, baby. Don't make me drop it in the low side." He fingered the lever on the shifter. Usually he could crest Chicory Mountain in the high side of the tranny, but today she had her tongue hanging on the ground and still felt sluggish.

He'd just decided he'd need to downshift when a crack like a gunshot split the air. The cab bucked and jumped. The hood of his long nose Pete jerked up. He yanked the wheel to the right, but the motor sputtered and died, and the truck stumbled to a stop.

Turbo swore. He hadn't had time to get off the road, which might have been a good thing since the berm was barely wide enough for a skinny lady's shadow, and he had a line of cars behind him longer than Sunday's sermon. He swore again before yanking the yellow and red brake knobs out and checking for four-wheelers before opening his door and jumping down out of his cab.

He wasn't a mechanic, had never had the patience it took, but he didn't need the intelligence of a tree stump to know his motor had just lost her cookies.

Torque could fix it, but he had to get it there. Tough's tow truck was nowhere near big enough to haul a rig. But first, he needed to set up some safety measures so he didn't cause an accident.

A four-wheeler went flying around, close enough that its side mirror almost brushed Turbo's arm. The driver waved with one finger and laid on his horn for good measure. Like Turbo had chosen to have his motor blow up here and actually wanted to be broken down in the middle of the road. He clenched his fist to keep his own fingers from an improper return salute and opened the dog box where he kept his orange cones.

He set the cones up while several kind motorists began directing traffic so the more patient four-wheelers stuck on the hill behind him could continue on with their life.

After calling Triumph Towing, owned by a friend of his from high school, he called Torque as he unlatched the hood and pulled it back. Ouch. He closed his eyes and waited for the pain in his chest to subside. It didn't, just migrated to his head.

"Yeah?" Torque answered on about the twentieth ring.

"I'm sitting on the upside of Chicory. She threw a rod through the side of the block."

Torque swore.

"Yeah. Thing's junk. Actually dented the side of the hood. I'll need Tough to get on that, too."

"Bring it in."

"I've got the hook coming. Just wanted to let you know, make sure you'll have time for it."

"I'm swamped. But you're blood, and I'll make time. Plus, you won't have any problems tearing it apart. You won't need me until it's time to put it back together."

"Yeah." Turbo didn't have the patience it took to put a motor back together with the precision it required. He was always better when he was moving. Active.

"If you've got Billy coming, you'd better tear the driveshaft apart. Last truck he towed in here needed a new rear end once I got the motor overhauled."

"Frig." Just what he didn't want to do. Crawl under his truck in the middle of the highway. He wasn't even sure he had the right tools.

"Better do it yourself. Billy swore up and down he took it apart, but all the gears in the rear were stripped clean."

"Got it." He got off the phone with Torque and made one more call to a buddy with a rig who could come and take his trailer and unload it. The Gettysburg mill was still waiting for their feed.

By the time Turbo had the driveshaft undone, the police were there, with their lights flashing to keep the cars alert so his truck didn't get rear-ended, and so no one ended up hurt out of the deal.

It took another couple of hours to unhook his truck and get his buddy's rig under his trailer. It was dark when they pulled into Torque's garage, which was lit up like a high school football field on Friday night. Oddly, both his older brothers, Torque and Tough, stood in front of the big, open garage doors, so Billy stopped the tow truck in front of the right bay. Turbo hopped out.

"Hey, guys. I appreciate this." He smacked Tough on the shoulder, who didn't say anything. That wasn't unusual, since Tough never did say much.

"Well, we've got a little problem," Torque said.

Turbo blinked. Was Torque so busy he wasn't going to be able to stick a new motor in after all? But, no, looking over their shoulders at the empty bay in the garage, he should have been able to just pull in...

"What's up?" Turbo decided to play along. They were probably messing with him after all the times he'd goofed off with them.

"Our wives took us aside."

"Yeah?" Turbo had to admit his brothers, both of them, had loosened up and smiled a lot more often now that they were happily married. He was glad for them. Really.

"What do your wives have to do with my truck?" He looked at Tough. Surely Tough's wife, Kelly, wasn't still holding that whole kidnapping the pastor at their wedding thing against him? How was Turbo supposed to know the guy was allergic to peanuts? He would have washed his trailer out after hauling that last load of peanut shells if he'd known. Or found a different place to stow the preacher.

Plus, he felt bad, he really did, but come on, it wasn't like the guy died or anything. Just because their wedding was delayed for a few hours while the ambulance came and, well, okay, he might have popped his head in the dressing room and told Kelly that it was Tough on the back of the ambulance, and yeah, maybe he might have given the AMS driver a hundred-dollar bill to run the lights and the siren while they loaded the preacher. But that was actually more of a favor to Kelly because it kept her guests entertained while they waited.

He adjusted his ball cap and put on his best innocent look, which included flashing his dimples. He pulled his cheeks even deeper when he saw Kelly and Cassidy coming out of the office in the back. *Hell hath no fury like a woman...* He couldn't remember the rest of that little saying, but the first part seemed to be the applicable thing in this situation.

"Cassidy and Kelly, my two most favorite sister-in-laws in the whole world. Hey, great to see you!"

Both had their arms crossed over their chest. Neither smiled.

Turbo swallowed and tried again. "Cassidy, I was hoping that you and Torque were going to let me babysit this weekend. I just love spending time with my angelic nieces and nephew." Okay, he might be laying it on a little thick, because Cassidy's lips tightened.

"I still haven't gotten all the peanut butter off the ceiling from the last time," Cassidy complained.

"And I'm pretty sure it wasn't coincidence that the rinse hose on the sink was wire tied open," Torque, the traitor, added.

"My best party dress, dry clean only, got soaked." Cassidy crossed her arms over her chest. "And I happened to be holding a sleeping twin when I turned the water on to rinse my hands and almost drowned before I got it shut back off."

Turbo rubbed the back of his neck, which was burning. "Yeah. About that. I think that was your son. I don't typically have wire ties on me."

"Jamal said you got them from the drawer in my office." Torque's arms remained folded across his chest.

"He also said that you used Velcro on the dining room chairs to keep the twins in their seat." Cassidy's eyes were narrowed in a way that made Turbo's entire insides squirm like worms in a bucket.

"Which, to be fair, Cassidy and I both thought was a brilliant idea and we now have it on every chair..."

Cassidy bumped Torque's shoulder with her own. "But that's beside the point."

Torque wiped every trace of humor off his face. "Right. Completely beside the point."

"The point is," Kelly said with a level look, "My wedding was delayed, we were late for our flight, and when we finally got on the plane with thirty seconds to spare, we removed twenty-five pounds of lead from our carry-ons. Each."

"I can explain..." So, his innocent face was starting to feel like plastic melting in the sun. His dimples were definitely not working on these two women.

"Yeah, I bet." Kelly's foot tapped on the cement. He hadn't thought either of them were angry at him. They'd laughed at the time.

"I'd let you squirm, but Billy wants to be paid so he can drop your truck," Tough finally spoke.

Great. That sounded like a subject change he could go with. "Yeah, I've got my checkbook in my briefcase."

"But..." Tough smiled. It looked sinister. "Where he unhooks it is up to you."

"Huh? Oh, well, right in this bay is fine..."

"No." Cassidy narrowed her eyes. "You're not getting off that easily. You think it's hilarious to play your numerous pranks."

"And they really are funny," Kelly added. Cassidy elbowed her. It wasn't hard to tell which one was the lawyer.

"No weakness," Cassidy whispered.

Kelly nodded sharply and squared her shoulders. "We're not letting your brothers do one thing to your truck until we get payback."

"Okay," he said, a little uncertain. He glanced over at the hose. He didn't really want to get wet, but that would be an easy one. They could squirt him until they felt better.

"So you agree?" Cassidy demanded.

His eyes narrowed. Something wasn't right. "To what?"

"Tough isn't going to touch your hood..." Kelly began, in a tone that made the hair on the back of Turbo's neck stand up.

"And Torque isn't going to even put your truck in his garage..." Cassidy added in the exact same tone.

They left their sentences dangling. "Yeah?" he prompted.

"Until you agree to play Daddy Warbucks in Harris's production of *Annie*." Cassidy spoke sounding like the lawyer she was.

If a trapdoor had opened under his feet and he'd fallen into a pool of used motor oil, he couldn't have been more surprised.

"What?"

"You heard us." Kelly said, her lips twitching, probably at the gobsmacked expression on his face. "We're not letting your brothers do a thing for you until we've gotten payback. And that's it. Daddy Warbucks, or no deal."

Turbo called back his dimples and used the sweet, low tone that had always gotten his tough-as-nails grandma to give him anything he wanted. That she could afford. "Girls."

Their faces hardened.

He held a hand up. "Ladies. Ladies, please. I completely agree with you. You absolutely owe me, and I can take it as well as I give it, but..."

"No buts."

"Guys," he appealed to his brothers. "You're not seriously allowing your wives to rule the roost?"

Tough lifted one eyebrow; the rest of his body didn't move. "You didn't have to run across Pittsburgh International Airport at a dead sprint with fifty pounds of lead in your carry-on bags."

"I'm the one who stayed up all night with my daughter who was wide awake after being sprayed with freezing cold water." Torque tilted his head. "How'd you get the water to come out of the hose dark blue?"

"Objection. Off the subject," Cassidy said.

"Later," Turbo mouthed to Torque.

"Okay, so I'd love to be in this play." Turbo hesitated, but his nose didn't grow from the outrageous lie. "But even I know that Daddy Warbucks was old and—" he paused dramatically "—bald." He lifted his hat. "Not bald. Sorry."

"I can remedy that. In fact, I'd take sadistic pleasure in pulling your hair out, strand by strand."

"Kelly, really. After all we've been through together?"

"The stress of thinking my husband was on his way to the hospital on our wedding day gave me selective amnesia. I can't remember any good thing you've ever done."

"Your wedding was six months ago. Grudge much?" Turbo slapped his leg. Seriously.

"I think he needs to be in two productions." Cassidy said, one finger tapping her chin.

Kelly's eyes brightened. "An opera. Definitely one needs to be an opera."

Turbo wrapped his hands around the back of his neck and flexed his shoulders, trying to work out the frustration. He hated it when he got stuck in predicaments like this that he couldn't weasel out of. "You can't make me do this."

"Then you'll have to find someone else to fix your truck." Cassidy's tone brooked no argument.

Turbo dropped his arms and kicked the cement. "Fine."

"Excuse me." Billy took off his greasy ball cap and nodded to the ladies. "Relevant info here. Every garage in this area is working on a four-week backlog. The economy's booming, and skilled labor is hard to come by. You'll be lucky if your rig is back on the road by hunting season."

Turbo's stomach sank to the floor. But then his natural optimism took over. Fine. He'd agree to be in the play. Then he'd just cause such a ruckus that Harris would rather hire the devil than have him continue.

"Okay, I'll do it."

"If, for any reason, you wuss out of the play, I will personally take a sledgehammer to the exact spot on the hood that I'm going to fix." Tough's expression was dead serious, and he never wasted words.

"I will spend an entire night if necessary taking out the motor mounts, so the next time you drive your truck, your motor falls out." Torque's dark eyes glowered, reminding Turbo that he had spent ten years in the pen.

Kelly bit her lip, and Turbo felt a faint stirring of hope in his chest. She looked up at her husband. "I forgot it's a musical. Does Turbo sing?"

Tough lifted a shoulder. "I don't typically run with twenty-five pounds of lead on my back, but I figured it out."

"Turbo is the most resourceful person I know. If he doesn't sing, I'm sure he'll figure out a way to make it look like he does." Torque pulled Cassidy closer and dropped a kiss on her head. "Any questions, Turbo?"

Turbo shoved his hands in his pockets and looked at his brothers and their wives. He spared a glance for Billy, who couldn't keep the grin off his face. As soon as Turbo met his gaze, his smile got even bigger. "Don't know when this pro-duc-tion is, but I'm gonna be buying tickets and sitting in the front row. I'll be sure to bring me lots of rotten fruit to throw, too. Gonna be a fun time."

Turbo exhaled, feeling like the breath was being sucked out from the whole way down his toes. His sense of humor and ability to roll with things didn't usually desert him quite so thoroughly. It wasn't really the thought of doing the play; he wasn't the slightest bit afraid of standing up in front of people and making a fool of himself. Heck, no. That actually sounded like fun.

However, he might be a dumb truck driver, but even he knew that he'd need to spend time with the other people in the production, "reading" the script. He could fake his way through that. Probably. But Harris would be there. She'd see him, and it was just possible that she would somehow figure out his shameful secret. He could bluff his way through it; he'd done it more than once, but the idea of seeing disappointment, shock, disgust on her face... His pride rebelled at the thought.

Why did it even matter? It wasn't like he'd talked to her more than a handful of times since high school. He wasn't sure, but he just knew that of all the bad things that could happen to him, having Harris find out he couldn't read was really close to the top of the list. He'd rather have his blowed-up motor shackled to his ankle and dropped over Niagara Falls. In January.

"So, you gonna be Daddy Warbucks, or is Torque closing the garage and I get to sleep with my husband tonight?" Cassidy broke the silence that had descended.

"I'll be on the stage," he said reluctantly.

"As Daddy Warbucks," Tough prompted, knowing Turbo well enough that he needed to have the words spelled out.

"As Daddy Warbucks." It felt like a cage closed around him as the words came out of his mouth. He dug deep for his grin and devil-may-care attitude. "And Cassidy, you can sleep with your husband tonight. I'll get the guts out of my girl. Torque can take over in the morning."

"Get the hood off too, and I'll be over around seven with a trailer to do it up in my garage." Tough pulled Kelly closer to him, his arm resting comfortably in the dip in her waist. Turbo felt a little current of envy zap through him. He pushed it aside, surprised. He'd never wanted anything but the best for his brothers, and he was glad they were happy, and that was God's truth.

But maybe seeing how happy they were made him feel even more left out.

Cassidy nodded. "That's great. I'll let Harris know and give her your number. She'll let you know when the first practice is."

He could see already that he'd be losing his phone first thing. Like immediately. Maybe he'd chuck it out the window on his way home.

"Thanks, Cassidy. So happy you're taking care of it for me." He managed to keep most of the sarcasm out of his voice.

Turbo went to get his briefcase out of the cab of the tow truck. "Looks like you can take her on in, Billy, and let me know what I owe you." He'd worry about everything else tomorrow.

Chapter Four

The doorbell rang. Harris checked the time as she set her book on the coffee table and rose to answer. Who would be visiting at eight in the evening?

A quick peek through the curtain revealed Kelly and Cassidy, and Harris opened the door wide. "Something wrong?" Why hadn't they called?

Kelly bounced up and down with a huge grin on her face. "We've solved all of your problems!"

"Nothing's wrong. Can we come in for a minute?" Cassidy put a hand on Kelly's arm and gave her a quelling look. Kelly clasped her hands together and scooted in.

Harris's chest tingled, maybe in fear, maybe in excitement. Her friends would not be excited and happy if something bad were happening to her, but Cassidy's look seemed to say that her news might not be as exciting as Kelly seemed to believe.

Harris led her friends to her kitchen table and grabbed coffee cups. "Tea?" she asked.

"Yes, please." Kelly grabbed cream out of the fridge, while Cassidy opened the drawer and pulled out spoons. Her half of the duplex wasn't huge, but the kitchen was nicely done in ocean colors, which made the room bright and happy despite its small size. On a librarian's salary, she'd never afford larger, and since she'd never have children, it didn't really matter.

They settled at the small table with their tea in front of them. "Okay, I'm dying here. How have you solved all of my life's problems?"

The only problem she really had was the production, which was not really a problem, since it wasn't happening. She just had to call the rest of the cast and tell them. Which she'd been putting off because she'd gotten one script early and Camila had already worked so hard on memorizing her part. She wasn't the only one who had already put countless hours in. The scenery crew. The art department at the local high school. Even the old community theater who had allowed them to have the practices and production at no fee would lose out since they had cleared their calendar for this month.

"We found Daddy Warbucks." Kelly's exuberant excitement was contagious, and Harris found herself smiling, despite Cassidy's more guarded expression.

"Really?" she said, knowing that her friend wouldn't lie or tease her about something like this. "Who?"

Cassidy spoke quickly. "I think this is a really good thing, and I actually think it's going to work out well. So don't..."

"It's Turbo!" Kelly interrupted.

Harris stood. Her chair went flying backward, landing with a loud crash while tea splashed out onto the tabletop. There was only one person in the world with a name like that. "No! No way!" Her breath came heavy and hot, and her head spun.

"...overreact," Cassidy finished softly.

Harris squelched that tiny part of her that actually jumped for joy at the thought of being around Turbo and gave free rein to the much bigger part that was aghast. "Do you hate me?" They didn't even know all of her history with Turbo. She slapped her hands down on the table and leaned over it. "You want to see me institutionalized? Either because the man would drive me insane or because I'd strangle him?" She glowered at her friends. "He will ruin the production. On purpose."

"He's promised to behave." Cassidy told Harris about Turbo's truck and the blackmailing they'd done.

Harris allowed her lips to curve up. "Okay, I like the idea of beating Turbo at his own pranking game, but not at the expense of my production."

"You didn't have a production ten minutes ago," Cassidy pointed out reasonably.

Good point. "I think it's better to not have one at all than to have one that's a disaster."

"Turbo is a ham. I think he'll actually be an asset to the show." Kelly blew on her tea.

"Everyone will have fun, at least," Cassidy stated the obvious, since everyone had fun when Turbo was around.

Everyone but Harris, who would spend practices trying to keep order, looking up for buckets of paint over her head, and keeping an eye out for frogs and snakes, probably.

"I think more people will come to the show just to see Turbo." Kelly took a small sip of her tea.

"The fact that he's singing will be even better," Cassidy added.

Another good point. Cassidy definitely thought like a lawyer.

"The more people who are there, the more who will see all the pranks that he pulls. The production is live. We can't just cut and reshoot when Turbo decides to do something..."

"Funny?" Kelly suggested.

"Stupid," Harris said firmly. "*Annie* is not a comedy. Or a tragedy."

Cassidy gave Kelly another telling look. "Listen, Harris. We didn't have time to run this idea by you because we had to act quickly. But if you hate it and would rather not have a show, we won't be offended."

Harris thought of the months that she'd spent in the hospital as a child. She'd been able to watch TV and even play video games, but she'd been so behind when she was finally able to go back to school. A library in the children's hospital would be a start. She envisioned bigger and better plans eventually, with laptops or tablets for the kids, audiobooks and group projects, art and music... But it had to start somewhere, and the library was the beginning. Without *Annie* and the funds and interest it would generate, her plans were dead.

"I suppose the goal is to make money." She wanted the play to be perfect, but...

"Even if the play is a complete disaster, if people have a good time and feel like they got their money's worth…" Cassidy's voice trailed off.

"I'm expecting some big donors to be there. They'll expect the play to be perfect." Harris fiddled with the handle on her mug. "I know Turbo being in it will bring in a whole new subset of people, which I'm actually really excited about, because it could mean volunteers and other help for the hospital library, but I don't want Turbo to ruin the relationships and expectations that I've already built."

"I understand." Cassidy's serious eyes studied Harris. "I think Turbo does too. I honestly do." She blinked and looked away before her gaze returned to Harris. "That's why, first of all, you should make sure that he will promise to read his lines and study them. With you." She held her hand up in supplication. "You basically supervise him learning his lines, just so you know he's doing it."

Harris didn't move. That would mean spending even more time with Turbo.

Cassidy continued, "Also, I think it would be a really great idea to take Turbo on a tour of the hospital. Show him your idea for the library, the space the hospital has given you, and let him meet some of the kids that would benefit."

Kelly nodded. "That's a great idea. I really think that under his goofy actions, Turbo is actually sensitive and caring."

"He has a great heart," Cassidy said seriously.

Harris managed to keep from snorting. Barely.

Cassidy lifted her mug. "His truck's down tomorrow, so he won't be working, and the library doesn't open until 12 on Tuesdays, right?"

Harris swallowed. She wasn't sure she wanted to show Turbo, notorious prankster, the dream that was closest to her heart. The tiny attraction she felt for him made her vulnerable. She didn't want him joking and crushing her ego along with her dreams.

"Don't chicken out on us, Harris. We got you your leading man, you take it from here." Kelly gave the perky smile she was known for, and Harris couldn't keep from smiling back.

"I don't know whether to thank you or to think you're not really my friends."

"Thank us," Cassidy said with confidence.

~

AT EIGHT THIRTY the next morning, Harris walked into Torque Baxter's garage. She had considered dressing down. After all, she was picking up a guy who had worked all night and was probably going to be dirty, tired, and grumpy. But she wanted to say "professional" to him, making sure he realized and understood she meant business and this play was a serious undertaking.

So, her heels and business suit felt wildly out of place as she stepped inside. Which was expected and okay. She would feel much better when they were strolling through the hospital.

Two men she didn't recognize worked on the truck closest to her. They glanced her way when she walked in then did a double take.

"Yo, Torque. One of your wife's girlfriends is in here." The guy who shouted threw a thumb over his shoulder at the black truck parked in the other bay, hood up. Turbo stood on rails beside the motor, one hand on the windshield, one hand on a hook that was being lowered over the motor. He looked up at the shout, the whites of his eyes glowing in his grease-covered face. Lines of fatigue tightened his mouth, but he nodded at her before his attention went back to placing the hook in the right spot.

Harris walked over, her heels clicking on the cement and echoing through the garage. Careful not to touch anything, she stopped at what she judged to be a safe distance and waited while the hook was attached and Turbo jumped down. Torque appeared around the side of the motor, not quite as dirty as Turbo, and they closed the gap between them and her.

"Cassidy said Turbo would have a couple of hours to tour the hospital today?" She addressed both of them because she didn't trust Turbo not to blow her off and figured Torque would make him go.

"He'll be finished here in a couple of minutes."

"I thought I'd sleep first," Turbo said casually.

Harris's brows went up.

"Your crap doesn't work with me, man. You're the energizer bunny." Torque faced Harris. "He was up all night. I've never actually seen Turbo tired, but if he sits down for more than two minutes, he'll be asleep. Just a warning. You'll need an atomic bomb and a supercharged cattle prod to wake him up again."

"Shut up." Turbo punched his brother in the shoulder with a resounding smack. He glanced at Harris. "I'm gonna wash up, then I'll be ready."

"Okay." Harris tried to keep her face professionally bland and not dissolve into wide-eyed consternation.

"Have fun," Torque said to her, with one side of his mouth tilted up. "Keep him on a short leash. He won't act tired, but he gets a little crazy when he hasn't slept."

Harris swallowed. "Crazy in what way?"

Torque's lip flattened. "You're safe." His brow lifted. "It's like a rollercoaster. Buckle up." He gave another half-smile before turning and disappearing around the side of Turbo's truck.

Harris stood in the middle of the garage, feeling dumb. Where had Turbo gone? She looked around. A circle of chairs she hadn't noticed before over in the far corner caught her eye. A large wooden frame-type thing sat against the wall behind it. Four bespectacled, white-haired ladies sat in the chairs. All four sets of eyes were on her.

Harris blinked. The ladies were still there.

Harris looked around. Yes, she was still in the garage. She walked slowly over, wondering if the chairs and ladies were like a mirage in the desert.

They didn't disappear as she grew closer.

One of the ladies stood. Harris noted for the first time that they all seemed to be working on...sewing. The ladies were sewing in Torque's diesel garage. Now, she'd seen everything.

"Not sewing. Quilting," the lady who had stood up said. Harris didn't even realize she'd spoken out loud.

"Oh."

"I'm Beulah Roberts." She stuck her needle in the two patches in her left hand and held out her right.

"Harris Winsted. Nice to meet you." Harris shook the cool, bony hand.

"These are the other members of the Kicking Quilters," Beulah said, turning in her orthopedic shoes and pointing to each of the other three ladies in turn. "Betty, Angelina, and Alda."

Harris shook each proffered hand, although none of the others stood.

"We all have bad backs and knees. Grab a chair and join us." Beulah nodded her head at the small stack of extra chairs by the wall.

"I would love to," Harris said, finding to her surprise that it was true. "But I can't."

"Oh? Hot date?" the one called Betty said with a wink.

"Don't be silly," Alda said with a twinkle in her eye. "Modern women work. She's obviously dressed for a job."

Angelina nodded sagely. "Dates happen in the evening."

Turbo appeared on Harris's right. "Now, ladies, don't go getting all heartbroken, but Harris and I are stepping out."

"I told you she was going on a date!" Betty hit Angelina's shoulder lightly. "Just like that little Sissy Miller. Remember her? She would go out anytime, day or night."

Angelina nodded, tapping a finger to her chin. "Great dancer. Didn't she marry that boy from the railroad shop?"

"Wait," Alda said. "Turbo, you're going out with Harris? I thought you and I had an understanding."

"We do. You bake cookies. I eat them. Nothing needs to change between us."

Alda gave a sigh of relief. "That's good to know. I was just getting ready to poke her with my sewing needle." She grinned at Harris. "Just kidding. Turbo likes to flirt with me, but I've got my eye on a better prize."

"Better than me?" Turbo asked in mock insult.

Alda wiggled her brows. "Mr. Pollack. Now there's one hot specimen."

"As long as he has his teeth in," Beulah said dryly.

Turbo finished wiping his hands. His t-shirt might be dirty, but it stretched across his chest like a loving second skin. "Guess I missed the memo about wearing church clothes."

The ladies cackled softly.

"These aren't church clothes..." Harris shut her mouth. "We can stop at your place, and you can change."

"That's nice. You're not going to make me walk around the hospital in these? Great. Do I get to shower, too?" His teeth flashed, and the ladies tittered behind their hands. He waved goodbye to them and steered Harris toward the door.

"Hey, wait," Beulah called after them. Turbo stopped and turned. Beulah disappeared into the office and returned with a homemade loaf of bread wrapped in plastic and a quart jar of what looked like some kind of soup. "Drop these off at your gram's. She was under the weather, and I forgot to stop on my way in this morning."

"Will do." Turbo took the food items. "Thanks."

"Tell her we hope she feels better."

"You got it."

Harris waved at the ladies and followed Turbo to the front of the garage.

Chapter Five

Remembering what Torque said, she commanded, "Just don't sit down."

Turbo didn't seem surprised. "So, I have to stand on the bumper for the ride to my place?"

Harris narrowed her eyes and stopped. If she said yes, would he really stand on her bumper while she drove? Was that even possible? "Of course not."

"Great. I'm driving. Keys in the ignition?" He continued to walk for the door, stopping when she didn't follow.

"You're not driving my car."

"I'm a professional driver. Plus, you don't want me to take your dash apart and put it back together upside down and backward, because I think I'll probably have just enough time to get that done between here and my house. How fast do you drive?" He grinned. "Or did you change your mind?"

Was he serious? It was Turbo, so probably not, but did she really want to have to try to drive and watch him at the same time? She held up her keys. "Okay, you talked me into it. But don't go over fifty, and you'll need to put something on the seat." She tossed the keys.

"I'm on it," he said as he caught her keys in one hand and turned, striding out the door.

She followed. How could he be so filthy and so annoying, and yet so...appealing at the same time? When he caught her keys, when his teeth flashed in a grin, when he flirted with the knitting club that apparently met in Torque's garage, when he threatened to ride on her bumper...she was so hopeless. She shook her head, refusing to return his smile or allow herself to soften toward him, and followed him out the door.

Turbo stayed a few steps ahead of her, holding the garage door open with his elbow while she walked through then shoving the bread under his arm and opening the passenger door for her. At least he wasn't a total Neanderthal.

After he'd stuck the food in the back and opened the driver's door, he took the rag he'd dried his hands off with and opened it up, spreading it over her seat. It covered about half.

She eyed the exposed seat material. "You're going to get grease on my seat."

He stopped, hovering with his butt inches from the seat. "I can take 'em off."

"No!" She fumbled with the glove box. "Please wait. I'll just..." Grabbing some napkins, she spread them out under his butt, careful not to touch it. "There. Now sit."

Turbo settled into the seat, moving it back and down, but his legs still looked cramped. In her compact car, he seemed to take up all the space, making the area that fit her so well seem too small.

"Bet with this short wheel base, this thing does awesome donuts." Turbo shifted from reverse into drive. Gravel crunched under her car tires.

Her back teeth ground together. "I wouldn't know."

"It's not hard to find out." He grabbed the shifter and tightened his grip on the steering wheel. "Hold on."

"Stop!" Her chest constricted. He was going to wreck her car. They would both die. He hadn't even put his seatbelt on.

He paused.

Her hand clutched the door handle. "That is exactly why I should never have allowed you to drive."

"You've never done donuts, have you?" He said it like there was something wrong with her.

She crossed her arms over her chest. "No."

"Then how do you know you don't want to?"

"Because I don't want to do anything that might wreck my car." Like any normal, sane person.

"If we wreck it, we'll fix it."

"I can't pay for that," she said irritably.

"If I wreck your car because I'm goofing off while driving it, I'm not going to expect you to pay for it." He shrugged like it was common sense.

"That's easy to say."

"It's easy to mean."

"I thought you didn't have the patience to fix stuff?"

"No. I don't have the patience to do the precision work necessary to make a five hundred horsepower motor work in perfect tune. Little stuff like this, body work, where you're running power tools, isn't hard. I'd just have to use my brother's garage."

"It's just better to not have to do it in the first place," she said, feeling every inch the prim librarian.

"If it makes you feel any better, I've never even so much as dinged a vehicle doing donuts. Or anything else for that matter. If you know what you're doing, it's not a big deal."

She lifted her brows. "If you say so."

"I do. Tell you what. I'll not use your car to do anything crazy right now, but you're going to agree to come with me tonight and I'll teach you how to do donuts. In my pickup."

"I'm busy tonight." Eating, reading, and sleeping alone in her home.

He shrugged and reached for the shifter. "Hold on tight."

"Stop!"

His hand froze, and he looked over at her. She half-thought that he wasn't really going to do donuts in her car, but since this was Turbo, she didn't really want to take the chance.

She closed her eyes and took a deep breath. His scent, soap overlaid with oil and grease, an honest, manly scent, filled her senses. His flashing grin, his angled jaw, his laughing eyes all filled her mind behind her closed eyes. She shouldn't spend any more time with him than absolutely necessary. He made her laugh, made her heart race, stirred feelings that she didn't want to admit to, let alone deal with. And more time in his company would only cloud her better judgment. Turbo was nice, but he was not the kind of mature, intellectual individual she was looking for. She was not interested, and she needed to act like it.

"Okay. I'll go with you tonight."

His teeth flashed, reminding her of the big, bad wolf. "You're driving my truck, too, by the way."

She glanced down to make sure her jacket wasn't red. "Couldn't I just watch?" From the safety of the top of a nearby tree, preferably.

"You're coming, you're learning, then I'm taking a video of the prissy librarian doing donuts in my truck." He put her car in drive and pulled out of Torque's driveway.

"I'm not prissy." Oh, no. "You're not posting that on social media."

He grinned. "No way. I'd never." His grin got bigger. "What's the library's website again?"

She lifted her chin; challenge met. "Only the administrator can post stuff on the library's official site."

"Yeah? I'm pretty sure Shelly McConnell is the lady who runs the site."

"She is, and I'm sure you cannot bribe her."

"Don't need to. I hauled a load of sand in for the pool she and her husband put in last summer and told her not to worry about paying me, that we'd catch up sometime." He tapped his hand on the steering wheel. "I'm feeling like a little bartering might be in order."

She wanted to pull her hair out. The normal feeling any sane person had after spending more than two seconds with Turbo. "What do I have to do to keep you from posting that video on the website?"

"I'm not sure there's anything you can do that would be better than seeing that video on the website." He grinned, his hands competent on the wheel as he made a right-hand turn. "I'll have to make sure my windows are down so the tint doesn't keep folks from seeing that it's you."

He wouldn't! Oh, but she knew he would. And she couldn't do a darn thing about it. Her neck felt like Old Faithful before an eruption. Harris was so angry she could hardly see straight. She tightened her arms over her chest, buttoned up her lips, and stared out the window.

They pulled into a trailer. "I'll be right back."

Just because he didn't seem to expect her to get out, she got out. Still angry. An old lady came to the door. "Turbo, you visiting your old gram?" Her eyes went past Turbo's shoulder and landed on Harris, who hadn't started climbing the few steps to the little porch.

Turbo stopped with his hand on the banister. "Nah. I'm just dropping off soup and bread from Miss Beulah."

"Oh. That was kind of her." Gram's eyes went again to Harris. She moved to the side of Turbo and held out her hand. "I'm his gram, since he was raised by wolves and doesn't know how to properly introduce people."

Harris smiled, despite her anger at Turbo. "I'm Harris."

Gram's eyes snapped back to Turbo. "This is the girl you dumped that paint on."

Turbo shifted. "Maybe."

Harris enjoyed every second of his uncomfortableness.

"Hmm." Gram eyed her again. "Good to meet you, Harris. Glad you don't hold a grudge." Her housecoat flapped in the breeze, and she pulled it tighter.

"Go on back inside, Gram."

"Give me that stuff. I'm old, not decrepit. I can carry it."

Turbo handed it over. "I'll be back around to check on you."

"Thanks, boy." She gave Harris another look. "See if you can't treat this one good."

"I intend to, Gram."

Well, he hadn't gotten off to a great start, Harris thought to herself as she let herself back in the car. They pulled away, and she stared out the window. The idea that he'd put a video on the internet...

A light touch brushed her arm.

"Hey," Turbo said in a much softer, gentler voice. He touched her arm again, his fingers sending shocks of sensation up to her shoulder and down to where they tingled in her fingertips.

He stopped at a stop sign at a deserted intersection. He waited until she couldn't stand it anymore and looked over at him.

"I was kidding." He tilted his head slightly. "I didn't mean to make you mad. No video. I promise."

She stared in his eyes, knowing he wouldn't lie to her but not ready to forgive him for pushing her to the point where she got angry.

He shrugged. "I just always have all these crazy ideas that float around in my head. I don't even do half of what I think of. I was just spouting the idea out as it came to me. And Shelly really does owe me."

"You mean you have more ideas than the ones that you actually do?" Now that was about the most amazing thing she'd heard all month.

"Thousands more. My brain never stops." He looked at his hand resting on the steering wheel, and his voice dropped even lower, like he was confiding a secret. "Wish it did sometimes."

"You can control it."

His breath huffed out. "The same way you can force yourself to let go and relax a little. It's flat-out uncomfortable, right?"

She moved her gaze away. "Yeah."

He pulled out, keeping his gaze focused on the road. "So, I'm being forced to do this play, which is hard for me and, to be honest, is really making me squirm. Maybe I just wanted to push you a little. Make you as uncomfortable as I am." He lifted a shoulder.

"I see." She met his eyes once more for a quick second, as serious as she'd ever seen him. Her heart melted, just a little. Her voice softened. "Misery loves company?"

He lifted his hat and ran a hand through his hair before settling it back on his head, keeping the wheel steady with his knee. "Yeah, I guess." His hand gripped the steering wheel once more.

She had to toughen up—this was Turbo—and take advantage of his weakness. She pushed the softening feelings aside. "So, you'll come to my house tonight after the library closes, we'll work on your lines some, and then we'll take your truck and you'll teach me to do something dumb that is dangerous and makes no sense, and that will make you happy?"

He lifted a brow. "Maybe there's a subset of people that thinks that plays are dumb and make no sense."

She wasn't giving him that point. Not yet. "At least they're not dangerous."

"I've heard of actors dying on set." He tilted his head. "They could get so nervous that they give themselves a heart attack."

She shook her head, laughing a little. "That's a stretch. But I do see your point."

He pulled into his house, a small blue ranch on a quiet, treelined street set back from the road. "It'll just take me a few minutes to grab a shower. Come on in." Unfolding his legs, he managed to unpack himself and squeeze out of her car.

She thought of just sitting in the car and waiting, but the little peek that she'd had under Turbo's laughing exterior had left her wanting to know more. Not because she had feelings for him, but because she was curious. She got out and followed him down the walk and around the side of his house.

He opened the back door.

"You don't lock your house?" The question was out of her mouth before she thought about it.

"Nah. There's nothing worth stealing in here anyway."

She blinked and took a second to swallow that before following him across the threshold and into his home. "But you do lock it at night before you go to bed, right?"

"No." He paused halfway through the bare kitchen. "Why? It's not like I carry my valuables around with me and put them on my nightstand before I go to bed."

"But someone might come in and...hurt you."

His brows furrowed, and his face registered true confusion. "Why?"

"Because there's bad people in the world."

"I know that." He rolled his eyes and stepped back toward her. "But, come on. Just think about it with me for a minute. Do you think thieves or killers or whoever it is that you're afraid of actually try the front door? You think they walk down the street, checking doors, and find one that's open. Then they're like, okay, this is the guy we're going to kill tonight, cause his door's unlocked. Seriously? I leave my door unlocked, and I'd bet a boatload of money that if anyone ever did decide to come into my house to hurt me or kill me or steal or whatever, they break in anyway. Bust a window or whatever. They're not going to check the door first to see if it's unlocked."

Harris just stared at him. He had a point. "So you've thought about this?"

Turbo shrugged and grinned. "Nah. I seriously don't want the bother of keeping the key. I made the rest of that up just now."

Harris smiled and met his eyes, and it was like the sight of her smile electrified him. His eyes crinkled, and his grin became a full-on beaming smile. "Holy frig, it makes me feel good to see you smile," he said softly. Then he shook his head, as though remembering who she was and where they were. "Make yourself at home." He waved at the open area in front of her. "There's water in the fridge and a couch right there. I'll be back in a few."

"Have you eaten?"

He stopped and popped his head back around the corner. His brows scrunched up. "No. I guess I haven't." He tilted his head. "I had two hot dogs yesterday morning when I fueled."

"You were up all night, and you haven't eaten since yesterday morning?" Maternal instincts that she didn't even know she possessed kicked into high gear. "You need to eat." She walked to the fridge and opened it. Empty. Not even a ketchup bottle. She spun around to face him. "How was I supposed to grab a water and sit on the couch when there is no water? What do you even have this thing for?" Maybe there was no couch, either. She hadn't made it that far into his house.

"Came with the house. Faucet works."

"Do you have cups?"

He dropped his hand from the wall and walked to the cupboard. A half-empty package of plastic cups and a stack of cheap paper plates were all that were in it. He pulled out a cup, turned the tap on, and filled it up. "Here you go."

"Thanks," she said, with a heavy dose of sarcasm. "So, you never eat at your house?"

He took his hat off and ran a hand through his hair. "I'm in the truck all week. When I'm here on the weekend, I'm too busy thinking about other things to think about eating."

"You don't notice that you're hungry?"

He shrugged. "Now that you mention it. But until you said something...no. I had other things on my mind."

"I'd cook you breakfast, but..." She waved toward the empty refrigerator.

"It's okay, Harris. It's America. It's pretty much impossible to starve to death. Even I'm not *that* resourceful." He slapped the wall and walked around the corner.

Harris sipped her water, walked over to the arched doorway, and contemplated the living room. There was a couch. Not a book or paper or magazine in sight. Just...she wasn't even sure what that was sitting in the middle of the floor. A big, black metal thing with pieces and parts lay scattered around a plastic sheet that covered most of the carpet.

Turbo considered himself resourceful. Interesting. Is that what one called it? She might have called him a prankster. Or...or what? Handsome. Funny. Unique. Definitely unique. In her experience, she'd never met a man like Turbo. Always laughing, always making other people laugh. His brain constantly in motion. ADHD for sure. She'd never really understood those little boys that came into the library and couldn't be still or quiet. Yet, she'd bet the house that Turbo had been a little boy just like that.

He hadn't turned out too bad.

Chapter Six

Typically Turbo didn't pay much attention to his home or think about how it looked. He always had a million things going through his head—business plans, prank plans, people he wanted to see, and things that needed to be fixed or made. But today, as he showered, his thoughts were on his house. Or, more specifically, what Harris might be thinking of his house.

The bare kitchen hadn't impressed her. Ha. She'd been shocked and dismayed by his empty fridge—when was the last time he'd even opened it? And by his bare cupboards. Probably normal people had a coffeemaker on the counter or his gram had a toaster and some containers with green lids. He wasn't sure what was in them. Kitchen stuff. He had a stove, but he couldn't say for sure if it even worked. He'd never tried to turn it on.

Man, she had to think he was pathetic. But the kitchen wasn't the worst part of his house. He'd never even considered what she might think when she saw what he was doing in his living room. He hadn't done much with it over the summer, but it was a project that kept him occupied after he'd visited the nursing home and played video games with DeShaun and a couple of other kids in the winter when it was too dark to do much else. He only needed about four, maybe five hours of sleep at night, and his mind ran too fast to lie in bed.

Harris probably wasn't expecting to see about half of the pieces of a 1945 Studebaker sitting on plastic in his living room.

~

TURBO DIDN'T MENTION the car parts. He didn't mention much of anything before they separated and drove their own vehicles to the hospital.

He shouldn't care what she thought. It shouldn't matter because as much as her smile thrilled him to the very depths of his soul, and as much as he wanted to make her happy like he'd never wanted to make anyone happy before, the studious, serious librarian would never take a second look at the likes of him. He knew it in high school, and life hadn't suddenly changed in the last decade or so.

He pulled into the gas station at the bottom of Hospital Hill. She followed him into the parking lot and pulled her little car beside his pickup. He jogged over to her window, and she slid it down. "I'm gonna run in and grab a couple slices of pizza, just to keep a certain person from feeling like they need to turn my kitchen into a five-star restaurant." He grinned, and his heart thrilled when the edges of her lips turned up. "Want anything?"

"A water, please."

"Okay."

The store wasn't busy. He had the clerk just hand him the pizza, and he shoved a water in his back pocket for him and carried hers.

"Here you go." He handed her the ice-cold bottle and took a big bite of pizza.

She looked at the pizza in his hand, her eyes wide open and her mouth hanging down. "That looks like it's about six days old."

He chewed, trying to look thoughtfully at the pizza in his hand. How could she tell? He swallowed. "That's a bad thing, right?"

"Doesn't it taste like cardboard?"

"Not really. Cardboard is actually surprisingly good. If you put salt on it, it's really not bad. Some of that green stuff, like oregano or basil or something, actually makes it taste pretty good."

She narrowed her eyes. "You're kidding, right?" She shook her head. "That pizza is dry and hard, and I can't believe you're eating it."

He lifted a shoulder, unsure what it was about her that made him want to spill his guts. His smile was gone, and he said in a low tone, "When I was a kid, we didn't have a lot, and food was something...when you're hungry, anything tastes good. I learned not to care."

"Not to care about what you ate, or not to care whether you were hungry?" she asked softly, no pity in her eyes but a thoughtful consideration.

"Both." Man, enough of that sappy stuff. He slapped the side of her car. "I park around back of the hospital along the street. Keeps my truck out of the parking garage. It's also free. It's a little longer walk, though."

"You come to the hospital?"

"Yeah." He didn't go into the details of the grant-a-wish foundation he was a part of that periodically had him here, giving rides in his rig to anyone—kids or adults—who wanted them.

"I'll follow you."

He shoved the last bite in his mouth—now that she mentioned it, it was hard and dry—strode around, and got in his pickup.

He led her to where he usually parked, and they walked in together. Her heels were high and pointy, but if they hurt her feet, she never said. She rambled all the way about how the play they were doing was going to benefit the children's library and all the big plans she had for it. He didn't really see the need to have a play or the connection between the play and the library, but if she insisted there was a need and a connection, he'd agree, just because he loved seeing her more animated than he'd ever seen her before. Her eyes glowed, and she practically shone as she talked about the kids being able to read and providing books for them so they didn't fall behind and all her other plans.

He nodded and tried to shut his brain down, because he really wanted to focus on how he could get the elevator to stop so he was stuck on it with Harris. It wouldn't be hard, he'd just...

"Are you listening?"

"Huh?" Heat crept up his cheeks. "I was, but I did space out there, once we stepped into the elevator."

"Oh."

"You were saying that they've given you rooms..." he prompted, hoping that was close.

"Oh, yes." And she picked up where she'd left off, her eyes shining, her movements quick and alive, her vibrant hair sparkling. It looked soft and inviting. He shoved his hand into his pocket to keep from thinking about touching it.

They walked along the corridor, nodding to a couple of orderlies. As they neared the new children's wing, a middle-aged nurse in happy pink and blue scrubs rounded a corner. He recognized her but couldn't remember her name.

"Oh, hi." She looked from Harris to him and back and kind of laughed. "You guys are like the odd couple. You must be partnering for some good cause."

Harris's eyes grew wide. "Rachel, you know Turbo?"

"Sure." She nodded. "If anyone can make a child laugh, it's Turbo. He's here more in the winter, usually, and mainly when we have big days, like What's Your Wish Day, or the Christmas Festival. Every year, he volunteers to escort a girl to the Valentine's Day banquet." She tapped Turbo's arm. "It's a guaranteed good time if Turbo is there."

Turbo shoved his hand deeper in his pocket. He wanted Harris to think well of him, and he thought all this might help, but he didn't go around bragging about this stuff and wasn't used to being talked about. Everyone thought he was a jokester, and that kept him from having to spill his guts about his secret. It also gave him an out if someone needed him to read something; he could always make up a joke and end up getting them to read it to him. It worked almost every time.

"Wow." Harris narrowed her eyes at him. "You didn't say anything."

"You didn't ask. You were too busy complaining that I didn't have any food in my house." His joke fell flat. He hated it when that happened.

Harris nodded in acknowledgment.

Rachel touched Harris's arm. "You've told him about your library?"

"Yes. We're here so I can show him. He's going to be in *Annie* which we're putting on to raise money to buy books."

"Turbo's going to be in *Annie*? What, as Punjab? I thought you had Dr. Dennis doing Punjab?"

"Yes, Dr. Dennis is still Punjab. I lost Daddy Warbucks."

"You lost him?" Rachel asked with a raised brow.

"Ha. No, he got a better offer off-Broadway and had to leave right away."

"He and Miss Hannigan were the two that you had hired, right?"

"Yes, most of the other characters, aside from Grace Farrell, are being played by people from the hospital. The kids are especially excited."

"I know. I hear about it every day." She adjusted the stethoscope around her neck. "They're also excited for the library. School just started, and some of the kids here are anxious about what they're missing. Having that library stocked would be a huge blessing."

They said goodbye and parted. Harris was quiet, and Turbo hoped she hadn't gotten mad at him again. Seemed like that happened to him a lot. People got mad, and he wasn't even sure why.

"Why didn't you tell me that you already spent time here?" Harris finally asked, as they walked the last few feet to the door marked "library." The hall was deserted, blocked by big double doors that led into the new wing.

"I haven't been here all summer. I don't come on my own. They usually call me if they have a kid who wants a ride or like for the Valentine's Day banquet, if they need more escorts. I guess I take a good picture and I make people laugh. I'm not a famous football player or anything."

She looked up at him, her green eyes deepening to emerald. "It still takes time."

He stood close beside her, breathing in her scent that he couldn't name but made him think of intelligence mixed with sass and a touch of flirt. The sounds of monitors beeping and occasional shouts and laughter were muffled by the double doors.

Her eyes pulled him, trapped him, and he couldn't look away. Time seemed to slow, and he was hyperaware of her breath mingling with his, the glow of her skin, her glistening lips.

"Harris, I..." he whispered, unsure what he was even going to say, just wanting to be closer. His hand came up, and he touched the soft hair he'd been admiring all day. Her eyes widened. His heart beat fast and strong. His breath was shallow. "I..." *want to kiss you.*

What was he thinking? This was Harris, the librarian. The two of them would never work. It was only a matter of time, probably tonight, when she would find out his deepest, darkest secret. His pride wouldn't let him get close to her, not when she was going to feel sorry for him.

But for some reason, he suddenly wanted, needed, to know what her lips felt like against his. Wanted to feel the curve of her waist and the softness of her skin.

She swallowed, and her eyes closed even more. One hand came up and landed on his chest, curving and sliding until it ran down his abs, slipping around his waist. He wanted to close his eyes, but he couldn't. Didn't want to miss a second of whatever was happening. Harris touched him, and his whole body burned.

His hand moved to her cheek, cupping it, feeling the softness. He ran his thumb over her skin, resting it at the corner of her lips.

He couldn't do it. Couldn't kiss her when she would be repulsed tonight. It wasn't honest. Like false pretenses. Until she knew, he had to stay away.

Gathering up all the willpower he didn't know he had, he took a deep breath and reached up above the door. Yanking down the lonely piece of greenery that hung there, he held it up, stepping back. "Looks like someone missed a Christmas decoration. It's dangerous to let mistletoe just hang around anywhere."

Harris blinked. Man, he wanted to step into her and pull her close. Hold her while the dreamy look returned to her face. But it slid away, and she threw a smile on her face as she opened the door. "Humph. Is that what was going on? And here I thought there were some paint fumes or something that were making you dizzy."

Chapter Seven

It didn't take long for Harris to show Turbo the rooms. Two patient rooms and a waiting room had been converted to a large room with study nooks on one side. The shelves were almost done, waiting for the books she would purchase with the money they made from the play they were putting on in three weeks.

Her legs had stopped shaking, and she could breathe again by the time they left the library area and walked into the ward for a quick visit with the kids. Most of them were in their rooms, but a few hung out in the big social area. A couple of kids recognized her, and a few more yelled when they saw Turbo. They grabbed his hand, and before she knew it, he was on the floor using the toy trucks and tractors to make up a story about a lost truck driver and the little boy who saved him.

He lay on his side, one arm propping his head up, his long legs in clean, dark jeans stretched out. His scuffed but newish driving boots were crossed at the ankle. He'd put on a button-down shirt and tucked it in. The green shirt contrasted nicely with his brown belt. Not many men wore belt buckles in central PA, but Turbo pulled it off, looking natural and relaxed. Had he dressed up for her?

She watched him with new eyes. The humming attraction that she'd always felt for him had burst into song, amazing, loud, expansive song, out in the hallway just a few minutes ago. She had wanted, expected him to kiss her. He hadn't. He'd made a joke instead. Which shouldn't surprise her, but it hurt. She felt like the stereotypical desperate, love-starved, spinster librarian. Why would a man as handsome and charismatic as Turbo want to kiss her?

No. She shoved that thought aside. Why would she want to kiss Turbo? He was...she stopped again. Everything that she had thought about Turbo was actually kind of wrong. He was nice. And, yeah, he goofed off a lot, but he worked hard and spent a lot of time helping people. He'd had a rough childhood himself and had been working, without fanfare or putting on a big show, to make other kids' lives better.

Harris walked over and sat down beside Quincy, who had a notebook and a pen and was watching the younger children play on the floor with Turbo.

"Hey, Quincy. What're you writing?"

Quincy gave her a shy smile. "A book."

"Oh, wow. What kind of book?"

"Well, my heroine is in the hospital, and she's my age." Harris nodded. Quincy was one of the kids who would really benefit from the library she had planned. At fifteen, she was too old for the childish things provided to all the kids in the children's wing.

"So, what's your heroine's problem?" Harris prompted.

Narrow shoulders shrugged. "I don't know. Other than she might die."

Harris was silent for a moment. Quincy was writing what she knew, which was what the authors who came to the library to give lectures always suggested.

Turbo looked over his shoulder, one hand still pushing a truck down an imaginary road. "You're funny, Quincy. You should write a book that would make other kids laugh."

Quincy's cheeks grew pink. Harris hid a smile. Turbo had that effect on her, too.

"You really think I'm funny?"

"Sure. You read me that story you wrote last winter. The one about that teapot that wanted to be a truck. I couldn't stop laughing."

"Most of the ideas in that one were yours."

"But you put the words together in a way that made them beautiful and…what was the word that Nurse Kelsey said?" Turbo grabbed another truck and lined it up beside the first.

"Ironic."

"Yeah. It was really good, and all the teens who come through here love it."

Quincy tapped her lip with her pen. "I guess I could make this funny."

Turbo pushed off the ground. The kids protested around his legs. He looked right at Quincy. "I know you could."

The boys chorused together, begging Turbo not to leave.

"I have to go. Miss Winsted needs to be at the library soon."

"Do a magic trick," one little boy begged, before a whole chorus broke out begging for a trick.

Turbo grinned. Harris should have figured he'd do magic, too. "I just happen to have his old rag here." He whipped a bright, multicolored silk rag out of his pocket and shook it out. "I suppose I could maybe turn this into a puppy." He lifted a brow at Harris, while the kids yelled their assent.

Harris shook her head. He wouldn't really do that, would he? Just in case, she said, "No live animals in the hospital."

His grin told her she'd made the correct statement. Where was he going to get a puppy anyway?

"Miss Winsted says no."

"You could turn it into the Empire State Building," one little boy called.

"You could make it unhook this from my arm," another one said, pointing to the IV taped to his slender, white wrist.

A shadow flickered over Turbo's eyes, but he gave the boy a grin and a shake of the head.

"Make it disappear," Quincy called out.

"Ah, boys. The young lady said to make it disappear." He took a step and stopped in front of Quincy. "Hold it," he commanded.

She complied.

"Is it a real rag?"

She grinned. "Yep."

He balled it up, shoved it into his fist, twisted his hand, then opened it with a flourish. The cloth was gone.

Harris, sitting with her face less than a foot from his hand, stared with mouth agape. It really had seemed to disappear.

"Make it come back," the boys shouted.

A couple of nurses and parents stood by the side of the room, watching with grins on their faces. Harris figured they were probably pretty relieved about the lack of a puppy.

"I didn't actually make it disappear," Turbo said. "Miss Winsted has it."

"I most certainly do not," Harris protested. That was one thing she was absolutely sure of.

"Really?" Turbo said with a lifted brow, his mouth tilted up.

"Really," she said firmly.

"Hmm. So, if you actually do have the cloth, if I find it somewhere on your person, you'll...?"

She crossed her arms over her chest. He was not getting her to agree to anything crazy.

"We'll figure something out," he said with a twinkle in his eye as his hand came up. He opened it wide and flipped it back and forth, showing there was nothing in it. He moved closer, keeping eye contact with her, and touched behind her ear. She felt a whisper of a touch, then his hand pulled away with the colorful cloth dangling from it.

His dark eyes danced. The kids yelled and hollered.

Harris wanted to cry.

It was the same side he'd touched earlier when they'd been standing in the hall outside the library door. He'd been planning this all along and had planted the cloth on her then, she was sure. He might have even made up the part about the mistletoe, too. She didn't know anything about magic, but she'd seen his empty hand. It's what had to have happened, and she felt like a fool. Her stomach twisted, and the back of her throat ached.

As much as she fought to keep her face straight, her expression must have given something away, because Turbo's smile slipped and his brows crinkled.

She ripped her gaze away and stood, forcing Turbo to move to give her room. "You have my number, Quincy. Text me if you want my help with your story."

"Okay," Quincy said. "But Turbo is the one who makes it funny."

"You text Miss Winsted if you need me, and she'll let me know."

"Just give me your number," Quincy said, getting her phone out.

A fleeting look of panic shifted across Turbo's face. Harris thought she understood the issue.

Harris stepped in. "I don't think your parents would think it's a great idea for you to be texting a single man. We don't want them to worry about you more than they already do."

Quincy's forehead filled with lines, but she said, "Okay."

Turbo mouthed "thanks" to Harris before turning to the boys. "See ya next time, guys." He ruffled a couple of heads and did some fist bumping.

They waved to the nurses and said a few words to the parents who stood nearby. But as soon as they walked through the double doors into the older, quieter hall, Turbo turned to Harris.

"What?" He touched her shoulder. "What did I do?"

She twisted her shoulder away and kept walking. "I'm going to be late."

"Harris."

"I'm fine."

He strode along beside her. "The second I pulled that cloth out of your hair, you changed. You have something against magic?"

"No. I have something against you pretending to almost kiss me so you could stick it in my hair to begin with."

"Whoa." Turbo caught her shoulder and spun her around to face him. "That's crap."

She crossed her arms. "Really? You didn't stick anything in my hair when you touched it outside the library? And you made up the mistletoe thing?" She rolled her eyes, annoyed at her stupidity and even more annoyed that she cared. "Turbo, your reputation precedes you. I can't believe you didn't have it all planned out."

"I didn't."

She sighed and looked away. "But I'm more upset at me than you."

"For what?" He spread his arms out in frustration.

"For getting duped."

"Duped?" He drew back, his eyes wide. "Harris, I swear, you're dead wrong." He brought his hand up, just like he had in the room with the children, spreading his fingers and flipping his hand over and back, before reaching up to behind her ear and pulling the cloth out again. "There was no almost-kiss where I snuck it back, was there?" he asked softly, waving the cloth.

He stepped closer. His eyes moved over her face; his breath fanned over her. "I've wanted to touch your hair since high school. I don't know how anyone can see something that beautiful and not want to run their fingers through it." He shook his head. "It had nothing to do with magic, unless the fact that you stood still and let me do it was some kind of apparition."

Her heart thumped in her chest. She could hardly breathe. How did he do this to her? She swallowed through the tightness in her throat.

"You're the one who moved away," she managed to whisper.

"I'm still here."

"Earlier."

His lips quirked. "You're mad at me because I didn't kiss you?"

"No." She yanked her eyes from his and jerked her body, moving to go around.

"Wait, please." He didn't touch her, but his whispered plea gripped her soul.

She stopped but didn't turn, didn't look at him.

"There's something you should know about me..."

He was gay. She'd seen enough movies to be able to finish that sentence. She just couldn't believe it.

"It might change how you see me. What you think." He breathed out deeply, a tortured breath. He shoved his hand through his hair. "Look at me, please."

She slid her gaze over without moving her head, crossing her arms over her chest. "I'm going to be late for work." Whatever he was going to say, she was sure she didn't want to hear it. And she'd lost her focus anyway. She needed to concentrate on the play and making it successful so she could finish the library. Whatever was happening between Turbo and herself was a fluke that didn't need encouragement. No relationship between two such different people would actually work.

He didn't say anything, and the silence stretched on. Finally, he took a breath. "So, we're still on for four-wheeling tonight?"

"After we work on your lines."

"I think we ought to do the four-wheeling first."

"Lines first." She wasn't budging on that.

His shoulders slumped, almost imperceptibly. "Okay. What time?"

"The library closes at eight."

"Great. I'll be at your house at 8:30. I'll bring food."

"That's fine." She kept her face impassive as he turned and they walked out together. She wasn't curious as to what he thought would be a deal-breaker for them, and she was glad he didn't kiss her because she didn't want to kiss him anyway. Lies she didn't even come close to believing.

<h1 style="text-align:center">Chapter Eight</h1>

Turbo pulled into Harris's drive at 8:27. His pickup dwarfed her car, and he enjoyed not only that contrast between their vehicles but the fact that her car was all factory, while his pickup was pretty much all custom. Work he'd done himself. From the tinted windows to the large tires, lift kit, and silver-black paint job, his truck was his own creation. Normally no one else drove it, ever, but for some reason, he was really looking forward to Harris sitting in the driver's seat.

He grabbed the bags of takeout and stepped down. He'd spent a lot of time today thinking of Harris. Normally in the garage, he had half his mind on whatever job he was doing—today it was hooking the new motor up—and half his mind on pranks he could pull, ways to increase productivity, or new trucking lanes that could open, but today, ninety percent of his brain had been on Harris, how soft her skin was, the fire in her hair, and ways to make her smile.

The other ten percent of his brain was working double time on that —how to make her smile. He hadn't really been thinking of his truck at all, and that's probably why Torque had finally kicked him out of the garage at seven and told him to go home and get some sleep.

He'd gone home but hadn't slept. He'd been too busy trying to decide how deceitful it was to hide the fact that he couldn't read from

60

Harris and try to kiss her anyway. After all, she was a librarian. He knew what she loved, what she did for a living. He couldn't kiss her knowing she'd never be with someone like him on purpose. Plus, eventually she'd find out about him. His pride wouldn't allow him to make himself even more vulnerable.

When Cassidy had stopped in at the garage with the kids after work, he'd managed to sound casual—he thought—when he asked in passing if the fussy librarian had ever had a boyfriend. Cassidy hadn't even given him a strange look before she'd said that Harris wasn't getting married and didn't date. But the shadow that flickered across her face had hinted there was more to the story.

He intended to change that policy. He didn't even stop to wonder when that thought had occurred to him and when the librarian had stopped being someone he avoided and had become someone he couldn't stop thinking about. He also tried to ignore the guilt that plagued him because if he were successful in winning her heart, wasn't he deceiving her if she didn't know he couldn't read? And guilt because Harris deserved someone better than Turbo.

Stepping up on the porch, he nodded to the neighbor who was sitting on his half of the duplex porch before raising his hand to knock. The door opened before he could. Harris greeted him with a smile.

Turbo froze. She wore worn blue jeans, comfortably loose, with a soft mint green sweater that made her eyes shine like emeralds and contrasted with her fire-red hair. Her skin glowed, and the freckles scattered across it gave it character. He'd never seen anything lovelier, but for possibly the first time in his life, his tongue couldn't find a glib comment to tell her so.

His heart pounded in his chest. Sweat broke out over his upper lip. He tried to swallow, but his throat was too tight.

"You can come in." She opened the door wider, as though he were standing there because he couldn't fit through or something.

He walked into her home. "Home" was the correct word. Greenery interwoven with strings of lights brightened the windows. Cozy rugs, several comfortable chairs, and a serviceable coffee table with a wax melter lit on it made the living room feel welcoming. It smelled like fresh baked cookies.

"So, I think this is the longest I've been with you that you haven't said anything," Harris said as she closed the door then walked around him and led him to the kitchen. "You have some kind of prank you're trying to time just right?"

He held the bags up. "Just supper."

"You're thinking of a prank?"

"I worked on my truck all afternoon and only thought of two things the whole time."

"Wow. How to fix it and what else?"

A guilty grin spread across his face. "Something like that, I guess." It hadn't been anything close. He'd thought of Harris and how to get her to date him without having to tell her his secret or having her figure it out.

"Okay, so what you thought about today is a big secret, apparently."

It was a secret all right. It felt like they'd been on this subject forever. He needed to pivot. "You look nice." She smelled good too. A little spicy scent to go with the cookies on the wax melter. Maybe cinnamon. Possibly nutmeg.

She took the bags from his hands and set them on the table. "What would you like to drink? I have tea, water, coffee..."

"Water, please. Anything else will make me too hyper to concentrate. Especially with no sleep."

She stopped with her hands on the cupboards. "You didn't sleep this afternoon?"

He shook his head, pulling drawers out, looking for her silverware.

"You've got to be exhausted."

"Nah."

She looked him up and down. He was suddenly very aware that he'd dressed for her in a similar outfit to what he wore to the hospital. He normally did t-shirt and jeans. Work boots. But he'd even worn his good church boots today along with new jeans and a button-down shirt. Man, he'd gotten it bad. He'd never dressed up for a girl. But Harris wasn't just any girl.

They spread the food on the table and ate without much conversation. This new feeling like his stomach had spiders in it was odd. It must be nerves. Strange because he couldn't remember ever being nervous before. The urge to make random, silly comments was almost overwhelming. He kept his mouth full so he wouldn't be tempted to say something arbitrary and stupid.

"You're awful quiet tonight. You must be tired and not even realizing it," she said thoughtfully as they finished eating.

Turbo stood, gathering up their trash and carrying it to the garbage can. His quietness had nothing to do with being tired. But maybe it was good that she thought that.

A few minutes later and the small table was cleared. She walked to the living room, picking up two folders from her neat, uncluttered desk in the corner. He stared at the folder she tried to hand him.

"I was thinking about this," he started.

"You've changed your mind?" she said immediately, like she'd been expecting it. He tried not to be offended that she had such little faith in him. He probably deserved it. It wasn't the first time in his life, but it was the strongest time, he wished he could be a better man. That the things he had to hide and compensate for didn't dictate the way others saw him. That his pride didn't run his life.

"No," he said more forcefully than he intended. He took the folder she offered but didn't open it. It was now or never. But old habits died hard, and he didn't even need to try to work this. He took a breath. "I memorize things better when I hear them and when I'm moving, so I was hoping you'd read my lines while I pace, and I can just go ahead and get started memorizing." Nothing he said was a lie, but guilt balled up in his chest like a traffic jam on the freeway.

"Well, you've seen the movie, right?"

"What movie?"

"*Annie*?"

"Two hours is a long time to sit still. I don't do it very often."

Her brows shot up. "That's a no."

"Yeah."

She bit her lip and fixed her gaze over his shoulder. He watched her teeth worry her lip and fought the urge to step closer and take the job himself.

Finally, she nodded. "Change of plans."

"Okay?"

She bustled around the living room, digging in a drawer and pulling out a case of DVDs. "Sit, over there." She nodded at the couch. "We're watching the movie."

He'd fall asleep. But he didn't say anything. He'd avoided the need to confess. That was the important thing. Plus, she said "we." Must mean she was going to sit...beside him. He grinned. That was something he could make sure of.

He strolled in the direction she'd indicated but stopped and pretended to study the stack of books on the end table. Thick, every last one of them. He'd bet there were no pictures inside, although the covers were pretty. They didn't look like anything he'd enjoy reading. If he read. Anything that required him to sit for more than two minutes would have to be supernaturally interesting.

Clicking and shuffling sounded behind him, and he turned to see Harris straightening. Graceful and slim, it was hard to take his eyes off her. She turned and caught him staring. He shifted.

"Sit down."

"I'm waiting on you."

"Oh, I'm going to sit here, in this chair."

"That's fine. But if you want me to stay awake, you'll want to sit somewhere you can poke me, or I'll be asleep within the first five minutes."

Her hands twisted together in front of her. "Well, then I guess I'd better sit beside you."

That was a win. Turbo hid his grin. Harris probably would take it the wrong way. He was absolutely serious about falling asleep. He could never sit still without sleeping, but it had definitely been a ploy to get her to sit with him.

"Why are you not smiling?" Harris asked suspiciously.

"I'm trying not to look guilty."

"What have you done?"

"Nothing."

"What are you planning?"

"Nothing."

"Then why should you look guilty?"

"Habit?"

She laughed and swiped the remote off the coffee table before scooting around and sitting down on one end of the couch.

He decided immediately not to overthink it and settled down next to her. Not too close, but not on the opposite end, either. "Am I safe here?"

"You mean, can I reach you if I need to smack you on the head to keep you awake? Yep." She gave him a sassy grin.

"Actually I mean my virtue. Is my virtue safe here, or are you going to jump me in the middle of the movie? Because if you are, I can move closer."

She laughed as the music started, and he considered it another win.

"What part am I supposed to play again?" he asked.

"Daddy Warbucks. He's not on for the first part. I'll tell you when you need to start paying attention."

Chapter Nine

That didn't go too bad, Harris thought to herself as the fireworks went off on the TV and the credits started to roll. At least he only slept through the first part. He looked like he was about half asleep now. Maybe she'd not have to go...

"Ready?" he asked, though his eyes were still half-closed.

"Huh?"

He grinned without moving. "We're going four-wheeling."

"I guess." She wasn't looking forward to it but had to let go of the idea that he might forget about it. "First...think you can do the part?" she asked, just to stall.

"I have too much hair."

She laughed. "You can keep the hair."

"You didn't tell me the part involved kissing. I'm going to have my agent demand more money."

"You should get less. After all, the lady who's playing Grace is beautiful, and you'll love her." Those words tasted bad in her mouth, but she said them anyway. Mia Babcock taught theater at the university in town, and a small amount of money had convinced her to play the part.

"What part are you playing?"

"I'm not getting up on stage!"

"Whoa." Turbo sat up, leaning his elbows on his knees. "You mean, you've blackmailed me into this, and you won't even do it?"

"I didn't blackmail you. I didn't even ask for you. Cassidy and Kelly informed me you were doing it. However they accomplished that was beyond my power."

He nodded his head. "I see. So, why not you?"

"First of all, I've been coordinating the scenery and working on the music and helping Camila—she's playing Annie—learn her part." She had paid for one script several months ago, just so that Camila would be ready. "I've been trying to make it so that everything comes together the way it needs to so we have to spend as little time as possible practicing. It's almost impossible to coordinate everyone's schedules for as many rehearsals as we need." She placed the DVD back in the case and knelt to put it away.

"Too bad."

He stood. She had to look away. The guy was way too appealing for his own good. Mia was single, and it wouldn't surprise Harris if Turbo and Mia ended up being an item by the time the play was over. Hopefully not until the play was over so she didn't have to watch. Although she would have to watch them kiss... She cringed. No way. She was not going to be able to watch Turbo kiss someone else.

Wait a second. When did that happen? She didn't care who he kissed as long as it wasn't her. Yeah. She slammed the door of the cabinet shut a little harder than necessary.

He held a large, calloused hand out in front of her face. "Let's roll."

"I hope you don't mean literally." She grabbed his hand and allowed him to pull her up, loving the feel of his rough palm against hers. She didn't want to let go. So she didn't, careful not to think about why.

Neither did he.

"That'll be up to you."

"I'd think you'd care a little more about your truck. It looked like you put a lot of time and effort into it."

"I did." He tugged on her hand, and she had a flash go through her mind. This is what it would be like, being with Turbo. He'd slow down for her, then he'd push her out of her comfortable complacency. She was happy where she was, but the excitement and challenge in his eyes was contagious. "I'm real picky about who drives it. My brothers. Me. You."

"Wow." She put a hand to her chest. "I can't take the pressure."

"No pressure. You can't screw up anything that I can't fix."

"What will you drive to work?"

"I park my rig in the driveway. I think I can manage to walk from my front door to my driveway a couple times a week."

Of course. She felt a little dumb. Not everyone drove to work. She didn't even drive to work unless it was raining or really cold.

Turbo made it to the door, which he opened for her. "You've driven a stick?"

"No."

He showed her that first. She was able to pull away from the curb, driving slowly down Maple Street, and get out of Brickley Springs, only stalling it five or six times. Basically at every intersection.

"I feel like I'm going to break something."

"You're not." Turbo looked relaxed and calm in the passenger seat. He had one arm stretched out over the back of the middle seat, one wrist sitting on his lap. He directed her farther out past the Brickley Springs limits. "Turn here." He indicated an old logging road.

"Are we going to get in trouble?"

"For what?"

"Trespassing? Or anything else?"

He laughed. "No. Trust me."

She flexed her fingers on the steering wheel. "So who owns this?"

"My brothers and I. We just had it logged a couple of years ago and use it for hunting, mostly. Although I think Torque takes his wife and kids camping a good bit too. There's a real pretty creek and an overlook back in. We won't go that far tonight." He glanced over. "Unless you want to."

"I'm reading the look on your face to mean that we can't drive there."

His grin exploded into a full-on smile. "You read right."

She wasn't real keen on walking through the woods in the dark. "Let's do these donut things first."

"The road takes a sharp left, then it widens out from the old log landing."

"Log landing?"

"It's where they bring the trees after they top them. They'll stack the logs, then the log trucks only have to drive in this far to get loaded. If they have tractor trailers hauling them, they'll have a loader sitting here too. A triaxle loads itself."

"I see," she said, but of course, she didn't. Not really. She'd never considered how wood got out of the forest. One got wood at the store. Just like milk, eggs, veggies, and meat.

"It's pretty dark now, but there's lots of dead wood lying around. I'm coming out early tomorrow morning to get a load of firewood for the Smith's, the elderly couple that live in the brick rancher on the outside of town. You're welcome to come too."

The library didn't open until twelve tomorrow. Spending this much time with Turbo could be dangerous to her heart. Too much more time together and she'd need to tell him her…secret—it wasn't really a secret, just something she never told anyone and which she had never even remotely felt like she'd needed to do with a man before. But she really wanted to say yes to spending more time with Turbo.

"We'll see." She gripped the steering wheel tighter.

"That was a yes." His chin was set with confidence. "It's getting light now around 5:30, so I'll pick you up at 5. It's best to do it when it's cool, before the snakes start to move around much."

"Snakes?" That could change her mind. Fast.

Turbo's relaxed posture didn't change. "I don't usually see any, although I did kill a big rattler earlier this summer. Eleven rattles and a bud." He grinned. "Don't tell anyone. It's actually illegal to kill them, but I had earplugs in because of using the chainsaw, not that I would have heard him anyway, and didn't see him until he reared up to bite me. I believe in obeying the law, but my reflex is survival. So, he got decapitated, I got a nice set of rattles as a souvenir, and I'm officially a lawbreaker."

She shivered. "Hmm. This isn't encouraging me to want to go tomorrow."

"It's October. I think they're mostly hibernating now." He grinned.

"You'll be fine. So, about these donuts...I think I'll hop out and walk around. You slide over, and I'll show you. I learn better by watching."

"Okay." She slid across the seat after he got out. Snakes, donuts, even just being in the woods at five in the morning, these were all things that she just never thought about and certainly didn't do. Turbo had brought a whole new dimension into her life. It was scary, but she felt alive like she'd never felt before.

He hopped in the driver's side. Confident. He grabbed the gearshift and depressed the clutch without hesitation, gripping the steering wheel like he'd been born with one in his hand.

"Start out in about third gear. I just know that from doing it before. Each vehicle is different, depending on their gear ratios and tire size. You want the tires to spin, so not too high of a gear, but you don't want to blow it up, so not too low." He grinned, his teeth flashing white. "Probably the worst thing that could happen, aside from losing control and hitting a tree or something, is dumping the clutch too fast and losing your rears or driveshaft."

"That sounds serious." His words came out too fast, and she didn't have a hope in heaven of figuring this out.

"We'll be walking home if that happens."

In the dark. "Oh, wow, I never thought of that."

"I'm kidding. There's no phone service here, but we'll only have about a mile to walk back to where we can call someone."

"So if we come here tomorrow and you get bitten by a snake, I won't be able to call 911?" Her stomach twitched.

Turbo looked relaxed and matter-of-fact. "Nope. But it'll take the ambulance 30 minutes to get here anyway, and in that amount of time, I can drive myself to the hospital."

She blinked. "You're not driving if you've been bitten by a snake."

"Okay," he agreed easily. Too easily. "Then you can drive me to the hospital in 30 minutes. The ambulance would be a waste of time. Plus, I'm not good at sitting around waiting for someone else to save me."

"I excel at that." No one but Turbo would consider calling an ambulance "sitting around and waiting for someone else" to save them.

He laughed. "Let's find you a new talent."

"I don't think it's going to be doing donuts in your truck..."

His hand wiggled the gearshift. "You never know. This could be a latent talent you just didn't know about."

"Somehow I doubt it."

He reviewed his comments about the gear and the accelerator then said, "Now, watch the steering wheel. It's kind of intuitive, but you have to be aggressive."

Aggressive wasn't exactly a characteristic that described anything about her, but she watched anyway, holding on as the motor revved and the truck spun left, shoving her against the door.

She kept her eyes on Turbo, though, maybe a little grateful for the opportunity to blatantly stare at him. His biceps flexed in the lights from the dash. His face was a study in concentration with his jaw flexed and his eyes constantly moving, scanning the area around the truck. They still held the laughter that was as much a part of Turbo as his slightly shaggy hair and strong, muscular legs. He looked amazingly masculine and confident. If she weren't pinned to the door by the centrifugal force, she'd be wanting to touch him.

"Now, the other way." Turbo let off, spun the steering wheel around, and gunned the motor again, slipping the clutch out and spinning the truck in a tight right-hand circle. Without the door to hold her, Harris felt herself slipping across the seat. She used both hands to grip the door handle.

He let off, and the truck came to a stop. "Think you can do it?"

She let out a breath and a couple of nervous chuckles. "Honestly? No way. I'll hit something, no question."

He laughed. "If I told you how many dents I've fixed in this old thing…"

"Old thing? It looks brand new."

"Means I must've done a good job with the coverups. She's almost twenty years old."

She grabbed onto the excuse, using the feminine pronoun as he did. "Then she's like an old friend. I couldn't stand it if something happened to her while I was driving."

"You did promise. But I guess if you're going back on your word…"

She eyeballed him. "I'm not."

"Then slide over. I'll walk around, but I'll sit in the middle, just so I'm closer, if you need me. Will that help?"

His presence directly beside her might be more distracting than helpful, but she couldn't actually say that, so she didn't.

He hopped out, and she slid across the bench seat, using the lever below to slide it up again so her much shorter legs could reach the pedals.

She could do this. It couldn't be that hard. Maybe if she just went kind of slow, that would decrease her chances of hitting anything. Of course, the truck probably wouldn't spin if she went too slow.

The door opened, and Turbo hopped in, sliding over so that he was sitting next to her, so close their thighs touched. Definitely distracting.

"Ready?"

Morose thoughts flashed through her mind. "Like a hog standing at the slaughterhouse door."

"Humph. Morbid." He shook his head. "Didn't know you had a dark streak."

She pursed her lips. "I'm telling you my feelings, and you're making fun of me."

Turbo slid his eyes over, taking a second look at her. He stared for just a minute.

"You're joking," he finally said.

She laughed a little. "Apparently I make bad jokes when I'm nervous."

He winked. "Laughter covers a multitude of sins."

"I think that's supposed to be 'love covers a multitude of sins.'"

His shoulder lifted. "Laughter works too."

"I suppose it does."

"You're stalling."

She couldn't argue. "I am. You're right."

"I love it when you say I'm right." Turbo grinned. "I'm also right when I say you can do this. Push the clutch in."

She complied.

"Shifter in third."

She struggled a little with that, since she wasn't sure exactly where third gear was.

"Nope, that's first." Turbo's hand came down and covered hers. "You can feel it when the gears grab. First grabs harder. It takes a little time to get familiar with the pattern, but eventually you'll be able to tell. Third is more to the right. Another way to find it is to go the whole way to the left." He pushed the shifter over, her hand still under his. Warm. "First is straight up from here."

Her whole arm tingled.

"Move to the right, just a little." He moved their joined hands over. "Press up, not hard, but enough to catch the gear as you go by."

Her stomach tightened.

She felt the gap and pressed up, just as the pressure came from his hand.

"Yeah, that's right. Just like that."

It slid into gear with a little thump. His hand rested on hers slightly longer than strictly necessary. Then he squeezed before taking his hand away. Her heart beat fast.

"Now. Turn the wheel the whole way to the left, press the accelerator, and gradually let the clutch out."

She turned the wheel.

"Press harder on the accelerator."

Swallowing, she complied.

"Let the clutch out."

Her hands sweated, and she gripped the wheel tighter. Turbo was beside her, and nothing was going to happen.

She let the clutch out, the truck started moving, and the steering wheel jerked in her hand.

"Keep pulling left," Turbo said in her ear, his voice a sane rumble over the screech of the truck.

She kept tension on the steering wheel. The truck moved in a circle. At the side of the headlights, she could see dirt flying up. The world spun around through the windshield. She made three or four revolutions, triumph bursting through her chest, before she picked her foot off the accelerator.

The truck stalled.

"Forgot the clutch," she gasped, shoving her hair back out of her face.

"Who cares? You did great!" Turbo said, putting his hand on her leg and squeezing. "Pull ahead some, and we'll get out and look."

She started the truck back up and pulled ahead a few yards before shutting it back off.

Turbo slid over the seat and out. She opened her door, getting out more slowly. They were in the middle of the woods, and it was pitch dark. Crickets chirped, and some other insect made a longish shaking sound. She looked at the ground carefully by her feet. Where did snakes go in the dark? Were they nocturnal? The dome light didn't illuminate much.

Turbo appeared in front of her by the open door. "Drop something?"

"I'm looking for snakes."

"Ah. I get it. I've got boots on, and it's going to have to be a pretty big snake that can reach up past my upper." He turned his phone's flashlight app on. "You walk where I walk, and you'll be fine. But I don't think we have to worry about snakes; it's too cold." He grunted. "I never should have mentioned them. Messes with your head."

"You did it on purpose?"

He laughed. "Nah. I'd mess with my brothers that way, but it's not fun to scare females." He walked slow, and she followed, determining if she ever did go back in the woods, she'd be wearing those thigh-high boots that women on the internet wore with fishnet stockings and leather body suits. She'd order a pair tonight when she got home.

Turbo stepped to the side and held his light up. "This is yours. Almost a perfect circle. Nice."

"Where are yours?"

He held the light up farther to the right, and she saw that his were actually perfect. They made hers look like the chef was drunk when he threw her donuts in the grease. "Isn't this disrespecting nature or something?"

Turbo shut his light off. Harris's heart jumped then took off running. Her stomach squeezed. She couldn't see anything.

"You ever see a buck rub?" Turbo's voice came out of the darkness.

"No?"

"When white-tailed deer lose the velvet on their horns, it must be itchy, because the buck will rub his horns against a small tree to get that velvet off. It can kill the tree. At the least, it takes a lot of the bark off. It's a natural thing."

Turbo shifted in the dark beside her. "Chickens will scratch an area until everything stops growing, and they'll make a dust bathing area for themselves." She sensed movement again in the dark. Maybe he shrugged. "I could go on. But, anyway, I guess some people think we need to worship nature. I think they have it wrong. You can respect it and still have fun with it."

"I see."

"If this were on a hill where we'd loosened the topsoil and a hard rain would wash it away, yeah, that might be a problem. But this is a flat area. We're good."

He was quiet, and she didn't say anything, either. She tilted her head. The trees all around the clearing circled the sky, but the open area directly above her shone bright with seemingly thousands of stars.

"I can't believe how bright the stars are," she said in awe.

He shifted again, and she said immediately, "Don't leave me."

There were a few beats of quiet hesitation, then his arm came around her shoulder. His warmth and strength flowed over and around her. She caught a whiff of fresh soap and aftershave mixed with the more manly scent that was Turbo's own. She breathed deeply, Turbo's scent subtle next to the spicier scent of the woods, earth, and leaves, full-bodied, and somehow calming. She moved closer to his body, tucking her shoulder under his arm and sliding her arm around his waist.

"I'm sorry. I must have a really bad rep if you think for one second that I'd bring you out here and leave you."

"I didn't really think that. Although, I guess it wouldn't have completely surprised me," she admitted.

He tensed beside her. She hastened on. "Not because I think of you as mean, but because you're known for pranks."

"Yeah." His chest moved beside her like he was taking a deep breath, and his arm tightened around her. She leaned her head on him and snuggled closer, not wanting to think about how right it felt to be cozied up with Turbo. It's not something she would have ever pictured on her own. Certainly the feeling of safety and of comfort, of the rightness of being beside him, wasn't something she'd thought about feeling at all, let alone with him.

She had been standing in the dark, just breathing in the clean woods air and listening to the night's sounds, admiring the stars and reveling in the comfortable solidness of the man beside her, when he finally spoke, low and quiet. "I'm not usually quiet and still this long, but I don't want to spoil the magic."

"Magic? What magic?"

"The magic of having this amazing and beautiful woman beside me. I...I never thought I was missing anything before. I'm never going to be able to come here again without wishing you were with me. And I'm not going to be able to drop you off tonight without wishing you didn't have to leave me."

Harris's chest felt like it cracked just a little. It hurt to think of Turbo alone, lonely. Wishing for companionship. And it felt amazing to think that she was the one he wanted. But Turbo would want what she couldn't give; she'd never gotten close to anyone, never led them on thinking that she was available for more than a casual dinner. Turbo had somehow gotten past all her normal barriers without her even noticing until it was almost too late. She needed to put some distance between herself and him.

He took hold of her shoulders and turned her to him. She couldn't see the features of his face in the dark, but his head moved slightly, like he was searching her eyes in the starlight that shone down. "I have to tell you something," he said, his voice low and rough.

She'd forgotten about his secret. But she didn't want to get into secret sharing, because if he told his, she should spill hers. And she didn't want to. Not tonight.

She placed a finger on his lips as he formed the next words. "No. Please no. Not tonight. Let's not ruin this."

His chest moved in and out. "I have to take the chance on ruining it, so I can have a shot at making it better."

"Later please?"

He sighed, whisper soft in the night air.

She asked, "How could this be any better?"

His chest froze. His hands tightened on her shoulders. All the night symphony seemed to fade until it was just background noise and the only things alive in the universe were Turbo and herself. Her senses were hyperaware of him—his breath, his scent, his warmth through the t-shirt under her hand.

His words seemed drawn from the depths of his soul. "I want to kiss you. That would make it a million times better. For me."

"Me too," her mouth said before her brain had a chance to stop it. Had she just said she wanted to kiss Turbo? She could hardly believe it was true.

His head lowered just a little. "But I promised myself I wouldn't. Not until you know something about me. Something that matters. Something that no one else in the world knows, but it will make a difference, I promise."

She'd read enough books in the library to know what would come next if this were a paranormal romance. "You're a werewolf."

He snorted then laughed out loud, pulling her to him, setting his chin on her head, and wrapping his arms around her.

"Nothing as easy as that," he said, still chuckling.

"You're a serial killer?" That'd be a book in a different genre but still something the hero would hide for a big reveal at the middle of the book. She was a librarian; she ought to know.

"No."

"My life's not in danger?"

His arms tightened, making her feel safe and protected. "No. Never."

"You're married."

"Frig, no." He sounded aghast, and she smiled at the outrage in his voice.

"Okay. Sorry."

"I'll think about forgiving you for that one."

"I was just trying to think of things that would be a deal-breaker for me. If you were dangerous." She hmphed. "I mean more than your constant pranks, dangerous. Or if you were married. Gay?"

His hands slid up and down her back, and he groaned a little. "No."

"Not married, not secretly a woman."

"Ugh. You have really low standards."

"Do you have a gambling problem?" she asked, only half joking.

"No. No gambling. No liquor. No porn."

"Gosh, you're practically perfect."

He laughed again. "Like I said, low standards."

She leaned back in his embrace, and he loosened his arms, letting her go. The darkness and the night noises felt comfortable now. She would forever associate night in the woods with this night and this man and these feelings. Peace and rightness. But desire lay there as well. She had to be careful.

"Then it doesn't matter. Whatever it is, it won't matter."

He took a breath through his nose. She couldn't see his face, but she'd be willing to bet the laughter was missing from his eyes. Sadness seemed to pour off him. She wanted to fix it.

"It will. I know it will."

"I want you to kiss me, Turbo." She shouldn't say it. She shouldn't go there, but the words were already out. She didn't try to take them back. They were, after all, the truth. But kissing wasn't the same as liking. Although, to her surprise, she realized she actually did like Turbo. A lot.

He didn't move. But his breathing stopped again. She smiled, that little detail somehow making her feel powerful and beautiful and desirable all at once. It wasn't a power she wanted to use against him, though, so she waited, comfortable with allowing him to decide.

"You don't know what you're saying," he finally said, his tone subdued.

"You aren't the only one with a secret," she returned.

"You have no secret that could make me not want to kiss you." His hands spread out over her back. She closed her eyes, enjoying the feel of Turbo holding her, relishing his strength.

"I might believe that. But a kiss on top of secrets could complicate everything." She paused, an idea coming to her. "How about this?"

"Yeah?"

"What if we just forget about all that. Forget your secret and mine. Forget that we're really not suited for each other anyway, and we definitely ought not to be standing here in the dark even contemplating the idea of kissing, let alone longing for it, as I am." She ended the last sentence on a breathless whisper.

"You sound like me. Aren't I the one that's supposed to say throw caution to the wind and just enjoy the moment?"

"You've already rubbed off on me. We'll have to stop seeing each other so much."

He laughed. "I think you just said I'm off the hook for Daddy Warbucks."

"No. I just said shut up and kiss me, darn it."

His hands came up and pushed into her hair. He sighed. "I'm not much for going slow, but there's so much about this that I want to just stop and savor. You realize how soft your hair is?" His thumbs brushed her cheeks, and his fingers slid down her neck. She shivered. "And your skin. I live in a rough world. I can't even think of anything to compare it to. Polished aluminum, maybe, but that's not romantic. It's just all I know."

Harris's throat had closed, and she fought to breathe. Every time he moved his hands, he sent fresh tingles down her spine. Her skin felt hot and cold, and her knees weak. He hadn't even kissed her yet, and she could barely stand.

"I want to see you. If I'm only getting one kiss, I don't want to waste it in the dark where I can't see your eyes darken or your face flush, can't see your lips glisten with my mark on them." He swallowed. "I'm waiting. You said I could kiss you, and I'm going to, I want to, I can hardly think of doing anything else. But not tonight."

Disappointment warred with admiration in her chest. If he wanted to kiss her as badly as she wanted to kiss him, yet he was waiting, he had some serious self-control muscles. It only made her love him more.

Whoa.

No, she didn't mean that. She didn't actually love him; she hardly knew him. She wasn't sure she even liked him all that much. Well, some.

His hands cupped her face. "What? What made your whole body freeze just now? Have you changed your mind?"

"What? Oh, no. No, I haven't. I didn't freeze." Her voice sounded high and squeaky, like an eighty-year-old sucking helium.

"Frig it." He lowered his head, and before she realized, his lips were touching hers. Soft, the tiniest of brushes. But it electrified her whole body, and she groaned, reaching up and gripping the back of his neck.

Her groan acted on him like spurs on a horse, and he crushed her to him, lifting her off her feet, one hand in her hair, one arm wrapped around her waist. Lights exploded behind her eyes, and she couldn't get close enough, couldn't get enough at all. She met his velocity, maybe exceeded it, until it was no longer who was kissing and who was being kissed. All she knew was she didn't want it to end, didn't want to let go, didn't want to face all the obstacles that would reemerge when they finally pulled apart.

Turbo was the one who eventually pulled back, allowing her to slide to the ground. "I know why people do this lying down, now. It's because my freaking legs are shaking so hard I'm not sure I'm going to be able to keep standing."

She laughed, her head lying on Turbo's chest, his heart beating hard and fast in her ear, and her own legs trembling. His arms were warm and hard around her.

"I'd say let's stay here. We could make a pretty comfortable bed in the back of my truck and could lie there and watch the sunrise, but I don't want you to have your neighbors whispering behind your back when I bring you home tomorrow."

"That doesn't have the stigma it used to."

"I don't want there to be any stigma attached to you being with me." She loved the care and protection he showed. His hand ran down over her hair. He seemed fascinated with it. "I suppose you hear this all the time, but you're one hen of a kisser."

"I don't hear that all the time." Especially since he was the first man she'd kissed in forever. "And I don't think hens have lips, actually."

She heard his smile. She could almost imagine the laughter back in his eyes. Her heart swelled, filling her chest until she felt like she could float.

"Come on, hon. You just rocked my whole world, and I'd better get you home before you jump me again and I end up comatose on the ground and you have to drag me back by my hair." He kept his arm around her as he walked her to his pickup and opened the door for her.

"I didn't jump you."

"I know." The dome light illuminated his smile. "You'd better not, either. I don't think I could handle it."

"Turbo?" She reached over and slid her hand against his cheek. He paused with one hand on the door, ready to shut it. "Thanks."

He put his hand over hers, turning his face and kissing her palm. "For what?"

"I've never been in the woods at night. It's wonderful." She met his eyes. "I've never been kissed like that. It was better than wonderful."

He closed his eyes and kissed her palm again, holding it tight to his face before he pulled it away. "I just want you to remember that I warned you. I don't want you resenting me."

"I would never resent you."

He gave her a look she couldn't figure out, before stepping back. "I hope you remember that." He closed her door and walked around his truck, and for an instant, she wished she would have allowed him to tell her what his "secret" was. He seemed to think it would really matter to her. It definitely mattered to him.

Chapter Ten

Turbo woke at twenty after four the next morning, ten minutes before his alarm was set to go off. He didn't wake up very well to alarms anyway. Understatement. He didn't wake up to alarms. He had to set his head to wake up. Otherwise, it took a massive amount of effort to wake him up. But he didn't want to miss his "date" with Harris. Even though he'd just dropped her off less than four hours ago.

He turned the hot water on in his shower and laughed at himself. This must be what being in love was like. An almost-obsession with someone. Couldn't stop thinking about her. Couldn't stop wondering where she was, what she was doing. Couldn't stop wanting to be with her. Couldn't stop hoping that somehow he could tell her his secret and she wouldn't be appalled. Or, the thought that was really going through his mind was that he could fake it, and she'd never know. That sat wrong on his shoulders. Heavy. But it was the only sure way. The other way opened him up to her rejection, which more and more was becoming something that would be unbearable.

At the least, she'd want to fix him. Maybe she wouldn't hate him, but she'd pity him and see him as someone that needed fixing. That would be worse.

Ten minutes later, he was out of the shower and dressed. He picked his phone up from the nightstand and was about to shove it into his pocket when a text from a number he didn't recognize lit up. It had come at one a.m., which was about twenty minutes after he got home after taking Harris home.

He tapped on the message, clicking until he got to where his phone would read it to him. Turning his bedroom light off, he walked out, listening. "Hey, Turbo. This is Harris. I got your number from Cassidy a while ago. I think it'd be best if I don't go with you tomorrow to cut wood. Thanks for inviting me."

By the second sentence, Turbo had paused in the dark hallway. His good mood and afterglow from last night evaporated.

She hadn't said why, just that it would be best. He listened to the message again, his chest roiling. He'd had an amazing time last night. He'd begun to think of Harris and himself as a couple. He'd even tried to figure out ways for them to be together.

Seemed like her thoughts had gone in the opposite direction.

Did this mean that she hadn't been blown away by their kiss? Had she been faking her enthusiastic response? Maybe she hadn't been able to find a nice way to tell him to get lost. He laughed without humor. Maybe she actually was afraid he'd leave her in the woods.

He shoved those thoughts aside. He'd see her tonight, since it was the first practice, and in the meantime, he still had firewood to get for the Smiths and a truck that needed to be completed and gotten back on the road. And if this was the way the wind was blowing, he'd be dipped if he'd allow her to see any weakness in him. He had to figure out a way to, one, not have to read his lines and, two, to memorize them without reading them. How hard could it be?

Chapter Eleven

Despite the fall chill, Turbo wore only a wifebeater with his jeans and boots as he chopped wood in the Smiths' side yard. Harris pulled in their drive, staring at the play of muscles as he lifted the splitting maul above his head and brought it down, making a clean cut as the piece of wood broke apart on either side. Harris swallowed, determined in her resolve to put distance between them. They were not compatible, no matter how much she was attracted to him. Yeah, she'd discovered that under his goofy exterior, Turbo was actually a nice man. A man of character and honor. But not for her.

She had simply decided to drive out before work to make sure there were no awkward hard feelings since Turbo had never texted her back. At all.

She picked up the angel food cake she'd made. After all, she couldn't just show up at the Smiths without an excuse. Turbo would never believe that she wanted distance if he thought she followed him around.

Another split rang out as she opened her car door and stepped out. Comfortable clothes were the order of the day since she expected to go straight to play practice from work, so she wore slim dress pants and a comfortable sweater under her coat along with flats.

Turbo's pile of split wood was much bigger than his unsplit pile.

She assumed he was probably almost done. She kept an eye on him as she moseyed up the walk, hoping to snag a glance, so she wouldn't have to walk over and interrupt him. The maul came down, and another piece broke apart cleanly. He reached over, grabbing a new piece with one hand, his fingers splayed wide over the end.

She wished she hadn't cancelled. It wouldn't have been torture to watch him all day. She'd have enjoyed it. Every second.

He looked up as he swung the wood onto the stump he was splitting on. His body froze before he slowly straightened. He nodded at her, his eyes wary, the normal laughter just a dim light. It made her heart twist to know she was most likely the reason for it.

"Harris."

"Turbo." With the cake in her hand, she walked a little closer, still leaving plenty of distance between them. She stopped and tilted her head. "You never texted me back."

He shrugged, standing the wood up on the stump and propping one leg beside it. He leaned an elbow on his knee. "Didn't realize you expected me to."

He didn't sound angry. She tried to decide how to approach him.

He spoke before she had a chance to. "I know I like to joke and goof off, and that can be annoying to people. But I shoot straight. I like you. I'm not pretending not to. I see a few things that might be roadblocks for us, and I want to face those things." His gaze was direct. His words even more so. "I got the impression last night from you that you felt the same way I did." He studied her, as though daring her to try to tell him that her reaction to his kiss had been faked.

She couldn't and looked away.

"I want to spend more time with you." He grunted and looked away. "Heck, I want to spend all my time with you, and I thought we were on the same page. Your text threw me, and I don't know what to think about it, didn't know what to say or how to respond. So I didn't." He waited until she looked at him. "There's no pressure. I don't want you to do anything that makes you uncomfortable or that you don't want to do. But I'm not going to lie, and I'm not going to pretend. Does that sound fair?"

Harris closed her eyes, fighting the feelings that rose in her chest and threatened to balloon up her tight throat. "I just don't want to make it awkward for the play. If there's some kind of," she took one hand from the cake and waved it in the air, searching for the right word.

"Romance?" he supplied with one corner of his mouth tilted up.

"Okay," she said. "Romance. If there's some kind of romance between us, it's going to complicate our relationship at play practice, it's going to make everyone uncomfortable. They'll think I'm playing favorites, or you'll think I'm picking on you, or you might..." She stopped without completing the thought.

"Go ahead," Turbo urged. "What are you afraid I'll do?" He waited. When she dropped her eyes and turned away, he spoke again. "You're afraid I'll sabotage the play somehow? That I'll get mad at you and take it out in my performance?"

"Or you'll prank it. Or not take it seriously. Or take advantage of me and my feelings for you."

He straightened and stepped away from the stump. "So you do have feelings for me?"

She sighed. All her life, she'd denied any romantic feelings. After her childhood cancer, not only could she not have children, but the chance of her dying from a reoccurrence was high. She hadn't gone searching for anyone, not wanting to put them through the possibility. If Turbo were different, maybe they could make it work. But she couldn't lie. Especially not to Turbo. Especially not after last night. "Yes."

"Don't sound so freaking happy about it," he said.

She smiled sadly. "I don't see it working."

He grunted. "You don't even know the half of it."

She whipped her head up. "Neither do you."

He left his splitting maul handle up on the ground and walked over to her. "I'll fight for you, Harris. I'll fight for us. Because you're worth it. So don't give me crap about what I don't know."

"What you don't know will change what you think you're sure of."

"It won't."

She swallowed, and her eyes drifted over his face, as serious as she'd ever seen it. His ball cap curved over his eyes; his wifebeater was covered in sawdust and dirt. His arms glistened with sweat, and his hands were fisted next to his strong, jean-clad thighs. His boots were spread apart and planted. She shivered. He was the handsomest man she'd ever seen, better than the heroes in her romance novels, flesh and blood in front of her, and he'd just said he'd fight for her. To have her. She should be swooning, rushing to him, wrapping her arms around his neck...but she couldn't.

"I don't want to jeopardize the play, and the children's library, because I went after something I wanted that I shouldn't have gone after to begin with." And once he knew that she couldn't have children and would likely die young, it would be the final nail in the coffin.

"I can respect that." Turbo's words were carefully neutral.

Harris's brain waged an internal struggle with her heart. It wasn't fair to push Turbo away. He hadn't done anything wrong. In fact, he'd done everything way too right. But she couldn't use the "it's me, not you" cop-out. Even if it were true. A man like Turbo deserved more. More than her.

He shifted. "So, I guess this argument started because I didn't text you."

"I just wanted to make sure the play is okay."

"Play's fine."

"You're still going to be in it?"

"Said I would."

"I don't want things to be awkward between us."

"Lady, I think you need some awkwardness in your life." He turned around, grabbing the handle of the maul as he walked by it, and walked to the stump. With one big swing, the billet sitting on the stump broke in two, pieces flying. He picked up another unsplit piece without looking at her again.

She should be relieved. He'd said he would still be in the play, said he wasn't angry and things should be fine. So, why did she feel like crying?

The angel food cake felt heavy in her hands. She didn't feel like continuing on to the Smiths' house and trying not to look like she was trying not to cry. She walked through the yard and set the cake on Turbo's truck, before turning and heading back to her car.

TURBO WALKED into the old theater just a couple minutes late. He'd spent the afternoon working at Torque's garage trying to get his motor wired up, which hadn't happened, and they finally figured out that they'd been sent the wrong wiring harness. Now there would be another two days of delay while they waited for the correct harness to come.

But he'd been filthy and hadn't wanted to show up at Harris's play practice looking like a grease monkey. So he'd taken the extra time to shower. He also hadn't wanted to do anything to upset Harris after their argument of earlier. He still hadn't figured out what she'd wanted him to text, unless it had just been something along the lines of he wasn't mad and wouldn't ruin her play.

He thought again of their kiss and the quiet bonding time holding her under the stars. Nothing had ever felt more perfect to him. True, his life hadn't exactly been polluted with picture-perfect family memories, but still. He knew a good thing when he saw one, and what Harris and he could have was a darn good thing. A great thing. It frustrated him that she didn't see the value in their relationship. Frustrated, but didn't surprise him. After all, even he didn't think he deserved her.

There were only a few people at the practice. Harris had said that only the main characters would be practicing for the first week. So the little brown-eyed girl sitting with her nose in her script must be the one playing Annie. Camila, Harris had said. She was a cute little girl. Made Turbo wonder what Harris's children would look like. Harris's and his. That thought should have scared the bacon out of him, but it didn't. Actually made him excited. He loved kids. Spent enough time chasing Torque's rug rats around, plus the strays he found wandering around the neighborhood that reminded him of himself as a kid. Wild. Unruly.

He'd never really thought about having kids of his own, but he could see it with Harris.

They'd have her bright hair and smart brain, maybe his smile, her drive and determination, his sense of humor...

"Okay, everyone." Harris stepped out on stage. "Daddy Warbucks is here, so we can get started."

A little jolt of nervousness went through him, but he shoved it aside. He'd prepared all day for right now. He'd faked it for years in high school. He should be able to handle a two- or three-hour practice.

He looked at Harris out of the corner of his eye. Still wearing the same clothes she'd worn to the Smiths' house. He'd taken the cake she'd left inside when he was done splitting wood, and they'd all had a piece before he'd left. Delicious. Hopefully their kids could cook like her too. He snorted out loud. There he was thinking about "their" kids again.

"Mr. Baxter. Is there a problem?" Harris stood on the stage, looking down at where he'd plopped in a seat in the front row.

"No, ma'am," he said with a straight face. He wasn't going to give her any reason to accuse him of sabotaging her play.

"Good." She sat down on one of the chairs that were arranged in a circle on the stage. "If all of you will come here and join me in the circle, we'll introduce ourselves and get started. I just wanted to do a readthrough today and mainly talk about some of the scenery, where we'll need to take breaks, and also where we'll need to deviate from the movie. For instance, there won't be the helicopter scene at the end, of course."

The other actors had gathered around, so Turbo got up too and hopped up on the stage. As soon as she said they couldn't do the helicopter scene, his brain had started conjuring up ways to make it work. They could do the helicopter scene. It wouldn't be hard. Ideas popped up like bugs in summer. He tried to shut them down. This had always been one of his problems in school too. He couldn't concentrate on the lesson, because his brain was never still and seldom quiet. Always deviating from whatever the teacher was trying to say. And the more he tried to suppress it, the more it felt like it was on fire. For Harris, he'd deal with the heat.

Another man and two women joined the circle along with the little girl. Harris waited until Turbo sat down before clearing her throat and beginning.

"I would like to start by introducing our two professional actors who have graciously agreed to be in our production." Harris nodded at the young woman sitting across from Turbo. Her long blond hair fell like a waterfall over her shoulders, and she gave him a worldly smile, full of promise. Her look made him want to look down and check to make sure his pants were zipped. He didn't.

"This is Mia Babcock. She is going to play the secretary, Grace. She's starred in several major productions prior to this. I'm excited that she's agreed to help us out."

Harris nodded to the woman beside Mia. "This is Aalyiah Cook. She's playing Miss Hannigan. She, too, has starred in several major productions prior to this and will also be a huge asset to our cast."

Harris smiled. "Beside me is Camila Sanchez. She's playing Annie. She has a personal interest in the hospital library, having spent more than a little time at the hospital over the years. And, man, can she sing." Camila's face broke out into a huge smile.

Harris then introduced Dr. Dennis, who was playing Punjab, and Jeff, who was playing Rooster, and finally Turbo, with no inflection in her voice. She also didn't meet his gaze but looked over his shoulder before going back to her notes. "So, let's not waste time. Next week, the rest of the cast will be here, and we'll have several weeks of practices before the weekend of the performance. If we sell enough tickets, we'll have two performances. One Saturday night, one Sunday night. Let's start at the top. I'll read all the parts that are not represented here."

Turbo closed his eyes. Crunch time. He'd had earbuds in all day and had listened to *Annie*, particularly Daddy Warbucks's parts, over and over. He'd done this in school and been moderately successful—good enough to graduate with a little extra help; he'd paid to have all his writing assignments done for him. Other people might call that cheating. He called it survival, with guilt.

It had prepared him for the real world. When he ran into a problem, say, like invoicing loads that he'd hauled, he hired it out. Of course, he was able to do some things himself. It took him longer and was a serious struggle, but words like Pittsburgh and Lancaster he'd seen often enough and could pretty much guess at. Sometimes he guessed wrong. That's where the joking came in handy.

When he hadn't been able to fake it in school, he'd created distractions. Harris would hate him if he screwed up her play, but he wasn't sure what was going on with her anyway. She'd been cool and distant since their kiss.

He'd almost been at the point where he'd have been willing to open up and take the biggest risk of his life with her. He'd never had a relationship that had gotten that far, so he wasn't sure how to handle it.

All his life, he'd had superficial relationships—come in the front door with one girl, walk out the back with another. They couldn't see his real self if he didn't let them get close. Harris was a woman worth pursuing and most definitely keeping. He hadn't suspected he would like her quite so much. Far more than any other woman. But his guard had to come back up. He couldn't show his secret to a woman who couldn't be trusted.

Harris began to read.

Turbo listened. Thankfully the dialogue followed the movie pretty closely. They skipped Annie's first song, which was a bit of a relief, meaning that he probably wouldn't have to sing today. Although he wasn't really worried about that. When he and his brothers were young, his gram had made them sing at nursing homes. That was before they'd gotten kicked out because he rearranged the decorations on everyone's doors, which started a bit of a civil war in the one nursing home because certain women had blamed certain male residents.

Then, of course, there was the rabbit incident where he'd taken two bunnies and a bag of rabbit food and placed them in a strategic—hidden —spot. The bunnies had babies before the workers had been able to discover their hiding places, and those babies had had babies before they actually called an exterminator to get the last of them removed. They hadn't ever actually pinned that one on him, but they still hadn't been welcomed back. But on the bright side, the residents had a blast talking about bunny sightings for months. Definitely brightened up the atmosphere of that home, which, with its black floors and low ceilings and small windows, had been the most dreary one they'd gone to. Tough had decided he'd rather die in a truck at a rest stop along the highway than ever get put in one of those.

He jerked out of his thoughts. Everything was quiet, and worst of all, everyone was looking at him. Crap. He knew what that meant.

Harris had an irritated, I-knew-you-were-going-to-do-this look on her face. He'd love to prove her wrong, but for the life of him, he couldn't remember the first lines Daddy Warbucks spoke.

He cleared his throat. "You know, I was kind of thinking we should strike this line out. It's kind of controversial."

"'I smell wet dog' is controversial?" Harris asked with one red brow lifted.

Turbo shrugged. "You know. Animal rights and all that. People might get upset if I imply that wet dog smells bad, you know?"

"No. I don't know." Harris folded her hands carefully and set them in her lap. Turbo's heart hurt for her because all she wanted was to have a successful play to raise money for kids in the hospital to have books to read. But he wasn't being a pain on purpose. "Are you going to read your part, or are you going to argue about it?"

He met her eyes. They were filled with disappointment. His chest constricted. He didn't want to disappoint her. It was the last thing he would willingly do. "I smell wet dog," he said, without taking his eyes off hers.

They continued on. He stumbled a couple more times, and each time he was able to come up with a smart-aleck comment to keep anyone from suspecting the real reason he wasn't saying the lines. He vowed to listen to the movie until he could recite it in his sleep.

Finally they'd made it through, twice.

"Saturday and Sunday evening, people who have songs to sing will be practicing from 6-10 with our music director and the small orchestra she's put together. I'll be there as well. I know I already mentioned it, but please make sure it is marked on your calendars. We have a very short window of practice, since most of the people in the production are normal people with real jobs. We need to make every practice count." She smiled. "Thanks so much for coming, and I'll see you all tomorrow night." Her smile faded. "Turbo, I'd like to talk to you after everyone else leaves."

Now he really did feel like he was in high school. It was hard not to adopt that attitude as well. He felt like slouching in his seat and crossing his arms over his chest. But this was Harris, and she might not know it, but he'd really been trying. For the first time, what someone thought of him really mattered.

Chapter Twelve

Harris hugged Camila. "You did a great job tonight, hon."

"Thanks, Miss Winsted."

After waving to Camila's mom, who was waiting in their car with her younger siblings, Harris closed the door behind Camila and stared at it, trying to contain the crushing disappointment in her chest. Turbo had acted out like an unruly schoolchild. She should have known that he wouldn't be able to take practice seriously. He'd interrupted the flow of the play, annoyed Mia, who was used to working with professionals, and made the rest of the cast laugh and look at practice as fun time rather than serious learning time.

A woman's peal of laughter interrupted her thoughts, and she turned. Mia. She'd thought Mia had left. But Turbo stood onstage, his foot on the chair he'd been sitting in, his arm draped casually over his knee. Mia's hand was on his arm, and she waved her other hand in the air, speaking animatedly.

Harris squelched her irritation. Yeah. That was Turbo. A flirt. Who had said that they'd never met the woman he couldn't charm? Well, she had a few things to say to him, and Mia could just get herself charmed some other time.

She marched down the aisle like John Philip Sousa himself were beating a drum behind her.

Remembering just in time to put a pleasant expression on her face—after all, she didn't want one of the professionals to quit—Harris cleared her throat.

Mia's head jerked around, but Turbo didn't look surprised at all, like he'd known exactly where she was.

"Oh, I'm sorry, Harris. I was just trying to talk Turbo into practicing the kissing scene." She fluttered her lashes in his direction before continuing. "He said he'd go find me a frog." She laughed again. "Isn't he funny?"

"Hilarious," Harris said.

Mia tapped his arm. "Don't forget, I'm grabbing a cup of coffee at the diner. I'll be looking for you to...hop in." She grinned, and in Harris's mind, her hand caressed Turbo's bicep three seconds too long, before she fluttered her fingers and walked to her chair to gather up her things.

Harris waited until the door closed behind Mia, using the time to gather her own things and make a couple of notes about what she thought they needed to work on.

"You wanted to see me, Miss Winsted." His voice came out low with just a hint of humor and defiance. It was also much closer than she expected.

She whirled. He was right in front of her. His chest a wall. She tilted her head. "I thought you were here to help. I thought you understood how important this is. I thought you were going to leave your immature antics for some other time."

Turbo opened his mouth to say something, then he closed it, swallowing, and looked away.

Good. He felt guilty for his childish and immature comments and actions tonight. But what really burned... Her mouth opened before she thought it through. "And if you're going to flirt with my leading lady, do it on your own time. Not here." There.

She didn't say he was a jerk for kissing her so sweetly last night then engaging in flirtatious laughter and meeting up with another woman tonight. But she wanted to.

His mouth opened again, and his eyes narrowed.

Harris braced herself, prepared for whatever smart comment he was going to come off with. He wasn't going to charm her. He wasn't going to ruin her play. And he didn't get to make her half fall in love with him under the stars one night and then come into her play practice the next evening and flirt with some other woman. She refused.

"I'm sorry."

She opened her mouth, ready to spew more at him. Her jaw hung there. "Huh?"

"I'm sorry. I know how important this is. For you and for the kids at the hospital. I don't want to ruin it." His dark eyes were sincere. "You're right, I did make some smart comments and disrupted your practice. I'll try to do better. But I wasn't flirting. She wanted to practice kissing, and I told her I'd get her a frog."

Harris crossed her arms over her chest. "And you're going to deliver it to the diner?"

"Never said I was going to the diner."

Harris raised her brows.

"I was going home and figured I'd practice my lines some." He shoved his hands into his pockets.

Guilt tightened Harris's throat. Why did she feel guilty?

"I'll help you." She wanted to take her lips off and examine them. Where had that come from?

"With my lines?"

"Yes. I'll come and help you with your lines."

Conflict raged across his face. "Nah. I'd better do it myself. Thanks anyway."

Harris's heart wilted in her chest. He didn't want her. She should have known, should have expected it. She'd tried to put distance between them, and she succeeded.

"But if you want to watch the movie again, I'm up for it." Some of his confident exterior had cracked, and the tilt of his eyes reflected his insecurity.

"I thought we agreed we couldn't..."

"That's like practicing lines, and you were okay with that."

"Yes, but a movie is more like a date." She checked the time. A little after eight.

"Then, how about this? Help me practice my lines by watching *Annie* with me." He grinned engagingly. Looking at his handsome face, Harris knew how easy it would be to fall under his spell. He was a genuine nice guy.

It was actually to her benefit to make sure he practiced his lines, so giving in this once wouldn't really count as a date.

"I'll bring pizza," she said.

"I like mine with pineapple and spinach."

"Seriously? We might not be able to eat in the same room."

He grinned. "I'm kidding. You already know I'll eat cardboard if you put enough salt on it."

TURBO ARRANGED the pillows on his porch swing and straightened the clean cloth he'd placed over the small, backyard table he'd placed in front of it. He'd figured Harris and he could watch *Annie* here in his backyard with his laptop sitting on the table. It was a little cool, but he'd brought blankets out.

He hoped Harris would enjoy sitting outside with him. She seemed to like the stars last night. He'd considered setting things up in the back of his pickup, but he'd decided to play it a little safer. For once.

Maybe he wanted to please her since he'd spent so much time during the play being obnoxious. Not on purpose, but to keep her from figuring out the truth. He'd not wanted to, but he didn't have much choice.

She had every right to be angry at him and to call him out about it. It was exactly the way he'd acted in high school. But, come on, once a kid gets to a certain age—like fourth grade—and if he isn't reading by then, everyone in his class is going to make fun of him, and he'll be put in the "slow" group and marked for the rest of his school career. It had taken Turbo exactly two seconds to figure that out. And less time to figure out how to keep the attention off the fact that as the class moved ahead, he fell farther and farther behind and got better and better at cheating and faking it.

Even if nothing ever happened between Harris and him, he wanted her to know that he respected her. But he had to do it here, because he couldn't do it at play practice. Not yet.

Gravel crunching announced her arrival, and he walked around the side of his house.

Her car came to a stop. He opened the door and grabbed the pizza from the front seat. She smiled at him. "Thanks."

"I have everything set up behind the house, if you don't mind."

"Not at all. Lead the way," she said.

He walked in front of her around his house. "Watch your step here," he cautioned her as he stepped up onto the porch.

"Thanks," she murmured.

"I have blankets, but if it's too cold for you…"

"I'm sure I'll be fine." She looked around.

He'd left a small lamp on in the living room, and it gave enough light through the windows to see by. Her face didn't show distress. In fact, she looked excited, so he figured he must have done okay.

He moved his laptop and set the pizza on the table. Then he sat down, unsure if it was more polite to let the lady sit first. But he wanted her to choose how close to sit to him. He wasn't exactly sure where he stood with her after her dismissal last night and his antics this evening.

She sat close but not touching. He'd take it.

They ate the pizza—the only topping was pepperoni—in silence.

"Is that your fourth piece?"

He stopped with the pizza almost to his mouth. "Maybe."

"It is. I'm just finishing my first piece, and you're on your fourth. Wow."

"I have three brothers, all older. It's a wonder I got any food at all growing up. I had to be fast."

She laughed, as he'd intended, and finished off her one piece. "Can I ask you something?" she said as he put the last bite in his mouth.

"Uh, sure?" It couldn't be a question he'd want to answer if she felt she had to ask him if she could ask him.

"Why did you do that tonight?" She looked down at her lap and pressed the folds of her skirt together. "I mean, was it because of today —me not going for wood? Were you mad at me?"

"No."

She looked up at him. "Then why?"

He pushed the swing a little with his foot, and the springs creaked. "I can't say."

"Can't? Or won't?"

Just tell her.

He wanted to. But for someone to whom words usually came easily, the three little words he needed to say stuck in his throat.

"Turbo." She turned toward him, her knee hitting his leg. She placed a hand on his arm. "Help me understand. Please?"

His chest felt like it was going to explode. His throat felt like a drain that was plugged and someone was sticking a plunger in it.

But the words just wouldn't come out.

He shook his head. "I'll try to do better." That was the honest truth.

Her lips flattened, and the disappointment in her eyes made his heart hurt, but she didn't press him.

They started the movie. Turbo put his arm along the back of the swing, and by the time Annie had snuck Sandy into the orphanage, Harris had snuggled against him.

Shortly after that, his phone buzzed. He'd set it on the banister. He didn't recognize the number. "Hey, I'm expecting a confirmation call about a load I had to cancel since my truck's not going to be fixed in time. I'd better get this."

"That's fine." Harris smiled, sitting up and pausing the movie.

He swiped the button on his phone. "Hello?"

"Turbo?"

"Yeah?"

"Hey, it's Aalyiah." She paused when he didn't say anything. "From play practice?"

"Uh, okay?"

"You remembered me from high school."

"Yeah." He could tell Harris was watching him out of the corner of her eye. How much could she hear? He switched the phone to his other ear.

"You hired me to write a few papers for you."

"Yeah." It was too late for her to turn him in, right? They wouldn't take his diploma. That couldn't be what she wanted. She didn't sound mad.

"Well, I'd gotten the impression, from you and some others, that... well, that you would struggle with things like reading and memorizing lines."

She paused. Harris straightened, her head coming off his arm and completely breaking contact. It felt like a big loss.

Turbo didn't know what to say to Aalyiah, so he kept his mouth shut. He'd pulled a lot of fast ones, and yes, he'd cheated some to pass each grade at school, but he hated cheaters and couldn't stand liars either. Any time he had a choice, he chose the truth. This time, he chose silence.

Aalyiah went on. "I thought maybe you'd need me to go over your lines with you. To help you learn them."

He glanced at Harris. She was studying her nails like she could really see them in the dark. He stood up from the swing and walked over to the edge of the porch. He pitched his voice low, trying to whisper without sounding like he was, to keep Harris from hearing what he was saying and asking questions.

"I appreciate the offer, but I'm watching the movie to learn them."

"Oh." Did she sound disappointed? "That's a great idea."

"Thanks. I don't think I'll need help. A few more days and I'll have it. Thanks for the offer."

"No problem, Turbo. You probably don't realize it, but my little brother was in the hospital a few years ago, and you took him for a ride in your truck. You let him blow the train horn and hold the steering wheel. It was all he talked about for days. You couldn't steal the smile off his face. It's funny, but that's when he seemed to crest the hump and slowly start to get better. Thank you for taking the time to do that."

"Hey, I enjoy it."

"I'll see you tomorrow."

"Yeah."

She ended the call.

He turned back to Harris.

"Everything okay?" she asked.

"Yeah. I'd taken Aalyiah's brother for a truck ride years ago, and she wanted to thank me for it."

"Oh." Harris nodded. "That was nice of her."

"Yeah. I guess seeing me today jogged her memory."

"I guess."

He walked back over and settled down where he was before, putting his arm over the back of the swing. She started the movie and settled back, maybe not as close as before. He leaned his head back and closed his eyes, willing himself to keep listening, focusing on the words as they were spoken, but a part of him basked in the companionship, warmth, and closeness of the woman next to him. He wished this could be his life. Snuggled on the porch swing every evening for the rest of his life.

Sandy and Annie had just entered Daddy Warbucks's mansion when his phone buzzed again. Harris shifted beside him. He grinned without lifting his head from the back of the swing. "Aren't too many times in my life when I wanted to be still. Figures my phone would ring, again."

He felt Harris laugh a little beside him. "Want me to get it?"

Reaching over, he grabbed his phone off the banister and, without looking at it, handed it to Harris.

"Hi, DeShaun," she said.

Turbo pushed his head farther back. He'd spent the time he usually spent with DeShaun at play practice and with Harris. Sometimes DeShaun was too busy for Turbo, but he'd had a rough start to his school year, and Turbo had been spending extra time with him. Regret pinched his chest.

"This is Miss Winsted, the librarian... No, I'm not Turbo's girlfriend." Harris lifted her brows at Turbo. "...No, we're outside... Sure, you can talk to him."

She pressed "mute" on his phone. "If he wants to come over and watch it with us... I mean, it might be too juvenile for him, but I don't mind, if you don't."

Turbo minded. He hadn't realized how much he would enjoy snuggling up with Harris and just spending time with her.

"I forgot I usually meet DeShaun and Pap on Thursday evenings and we do something." It wasn't like a set date all the time, and Turbo always initiated it. "I didn't realize DeShaun even noticed that was kind of my schedule. Friday's the day I always sign Pap out of the home."

"So, it's okay?"

"You mind going and picking him up and watching this at the nursing home with Pap?"

She tilted her head, a little smile lifting the corners of her mouth. "I don't."

"Then let's do it." He held out his hand for his phone. He unmuted it. "DeShaun?"

"Hey, man. You ditched me for a chick."

"Nah. I just got screwed up on my days with my truck down and play practice. I've got a movie to watch for homework for the play. You mind if I pick you up and we'll go to Pap's and watch it there?"

"Yeah. I'm down for that."

"You mind if I bring Miss Winsted?"

There was a pause. "She said she wasn't your girlfriend."

Chapter Thirteen

"She's not."

Harris had risen from the swing, closed his computer, and started folding the blankets. Her face held serene contentment. She didn't seem like she was disturbed about having to move. He supposed that was a good thing, although he wouldn't mind if she showed a little annoyance at having their cozy movie time interrupted.

He was sure as heck annoyed. But he felt bad too, since DeShaun was right. He'd totally forgotten about what he usually did because of Harris.

"Why you bringing her?"

"I think she needs us, bud. She's stuck in that library with all those books all the time. Messes with your head."

"Oh. Yeah. I can see that. Okay. I'll try to help her be normal. If you're sure she's not your girlfriend."

"Not yet," Turbo said with a grin. Harris either couldn't hear or wasn't listening, because she finished folding the last blanket and set it in a pile with the rest. "We'll see you in a few."

He swiped off and looked up. "You sure you don't mind?"

"It was my idea." She straightened. "Won't DeShaun's parents want him home at a certain time on a school night?"

"They're probably not home. If his dad is, he'll be passed out drunk on the couch."

Harris covered her mouth with her hand. "How sad."

"Yeah." Turbo shrugged. He couldn't do more than what he was. "You ready? DeShaun sounded a little jacked at me."

"You want to take the blankets along? We can make a cozy spot somewhere at the nursing home."

They ended up taking the blankets, picking up DeShaun, getting Pap, and making a makeshift movie theater in the common room at the nursing home. As they moved Pap in, several others gathered around, and it became a regular movie night. Someone made popcorn, which someone else complained about because it smelled so good, but it got stuck in their dentures and they couldn't eat it.

By the time Turbo and Harris had arranged all the wheelchairs and confirmed with the nurses that everyone who was eating popcorn was allowed to, the movie was started. DeShaun lay sprawled out on the floor, and all the couches and other seats were taken. A line of wheelchairs ringed the outer edges. Someone had hooked up Turbo's laptop to the TV because the screen was bigger.

"We can bring some chairs up from the activity room downstairs for you two," the nurse whose name started with a "J" said.

"You don't have to. Not for me, at least," Harris said. "I can sit on the floor."

Turbo threaded through the wheelchairs and grabbed the last blanket that had been thrown over the back of the couch. "Come on." He held it up. "I'll share."

"Would you two be quiet? We're trying to watch the movie," a silver-haired woman said from her seat on the couch.

"The TV is up so loud, I can't believe they can even hear us over it," Harris said.

"I can hear you just fine. You're worse than my kids were when I tried to watch my soaps," the same woman snapped. "If you can't be quiet, go to a different room."

"I think someone is up past their bedtime," Turbo whispered in Harris's ear.

She laughed and turned to him, her unique scent of books and smiles reaching his nose, tempting him to lean closer.

She grabbed his hand. "Come on. We can sit along the wall."

He allowed her to lead him over, savoring the feel of her soft, sweet hand in his. He tightened his fingers. She looked up. He stared down into her eyes.

She let out a little puff of breath, then her chest rose and fell faster.

He pulled on their linked hands, and she came closer. He wanted to put his arms around her and press her to him, but with all the people in the room, it wasn't exactly a romantic setting. Plus, she seemed to have wanted distance, even though it looked like she'd forgiven or forgotten about his behavior at the play tonight. It might embarrass her. He didn't want that, either.

Taking the quilt from her, he said, "I'll spread it out."

Giving him an easy smile, she said, "Thanks."

They sat down in the back, behind the last row of wheelchairs, on the comfy quilt. Darkness had settled outside the large picture window, which gave the dim room an even cozier feel. Annie sang and danced her way across the screen, and Turbo paid attention to the lines he needed to learn, but his whole focus was on the woman beside him. Soft and warm, sweet and generous. If only he could swallow his pride and confess. She'd want to "fix" him, sure. But it might be worth it.

HARRIS SNUGGLED against Turbo's side. Sometime during the movie, she'd laid her head on his arm. They'd both shifted a little closer, and now they sat with their sides touching as the credits rolled. She didn't want to get up. Something about being with Turbo made everything in her soul feel just right.

One of the workers turned the lights from dim to bright, and they started wheeling residents to their rooms. Harris shifted. Beside her, Turbo stirred, moving his legs and standing in one fluid motion. He held his hand out for her. She met his laughing gaze with a smile of her own.

"I'm gonna give the folks a hand getting back to their rooms. It'll just be a few minutes."

DeShaun was already up, giving his arm to an elderly woman with a cane in her other hand. Harris jumped in, rearranging the furniture back to the way it was and picking up pieces of popcorn and garbage that littered the floor.

They left the home not long after eleven and stopped at DeShaun's house. Turbo parked along the curb and strode up the walk despite DeShaun's protests that he was old enough to walk himself into his house.

Turbo was in the house about ten minutes before he jogged back out and climbed in the driver's side.

"I'm sorry about that." He put the truck in gear and pulled out.

"It's okay."

"I just know that sometimes if his dad isn't completely passed out, he gets violent, and it doesn't take much to set him off. I like to know DeShaun didn't set off a rage by being with me."

Harris narrowed her eyes at him. "You think DeShaun is abused?"

Turbo shrugged. "Kids are usually pretty protective of their parents. Even bad parents. He won't say. I've never seen evidence on DeShaun, but the guy came thundering down the steps a couple of times while I was there playing video games. Just the look on the kid's face...made me think the man's done more than yell at him." He took the turn and started on the road that led out of town. "I'd rather drop you off at your house, but we left your car at mine."

She stifled a yawn. "It's been quite a day." She looked at Turbo, who still looked alert and energetic. Did the man never stop? He'd been up way before her to get wood.

"I'm picking up my hood at Tough's tomorrow if you want to come along." His words were said casually, like he didn't care whether she did or not. But his fingers tightened on the steering wheel, and he kept his eyes on the road.

"Friday is actually my morning off. The library's staffed by volunteers tomorrow morning and Saturday."

He nodded but still didn't look at her.

"Will Tough mind if I come?" she asked, hating the little bit of hesitation in her voice. She wanted to spend time with Turbo, but after seeing him with DeShaun and Camila, she knew the fact that she couldn't have kids could make difference to him. She'd found out the hard way that some men were not the slightest bit interested in "raising someone else's child" as one man had called adoption.

She didn't want to postpone the inevitable—Turbo ditching her for a woman who could be a wife *and* a mother. Not to mention, things had already been awkward at the play.

"Nah. They'll tease me some." He glanced over at her, as though weighing her reaction to his words. "Somehow they got the impression at Torque's wedding that we didn't like each other."

"Understandable," Harris said, nodding in a way that she hoped appeared thoughtful and not embarrassed.

Turbo pulled into his driveway. "Yeah, I'm not sure if it was the fact that I had to forfeit the deposit on my tux because you dumped your juice on my head or the fact that you crawled under the table to get away from me."

Harris yanked up on her door handle. "For the last time, the juice thing was an accident."

"If you say so. Kinda funny how it landed on my head like that."

"The spider that you put in my drink scared me, and I jumped, accidentally throwing my arms up, and the drink slipped out of my hand and onto your head." Harris shut her door and walked around the front of the truck, meeting Turbo in front of the grill.

"At least your story hasn't changed." He leaned a hip against the front of his grill.

"It hasn't changed because it's the truth." She rolled her eyes.

"Then, you got scared and crawled under the table because you thought I was going to grab your neck or something."

"That's not true."

"That's my brothers' version of the story." Turbo crossed his arms over his chest.

"Did you tell them that I was on my hands and knees cleaning up the punch that mostly landed on the floor..."

"It dripped off my head."

"There was a small spot on your head."

"I was soaked."

Okay, so she wasn't going to win that argument. Most of her cup *did* land on his head, even though it *was* an accident. Mostly. "Maybe they thought we didn't get along because after you put the spider in my drink and after you mentioned that I should have been the one wearing the juice because it was the same color as my hair, you followed me under the table and tried to trade seats with someone three tables down."

"I wasn't trading seats, I was borrowing scissors."

"That was you! I knew it was you." She narrowed her eyes at him. "It's a lucky thing that Cassidy had a small, informal wedding, because if you had actually cut a piece out of an expensive dress... How... When...?"

"Haven't you ever seen *The Parent Trap*? The old one?"

She thought about the movie for a moment. "I never stood by the punch bowl."

"No, but I was under the table while you were standing beside it. You probably would have noticed, but you had a screaming twin in each arm, and I couldn't resist."

"I can't believe you cut the back of my dress out."

"I only went up to midthigh. I mean, I think I could have gone the whole way up as loud as they were screaming, but I didn't want to embarrass you."

"Oh, really?"

"Yeah, really. Unlike you."

"Me?" She felt a little twinge of guilt.

"Yeah. When it was your turn for the mic, instead of heaping praise on Cassidy and Torque, you spent the entire five minutes comparing me to Indiana Jones's pet monkey."

"The similarities were striking."

Instead of being offended, Turbo chuckled. "You did have every single guest laughing."

"No. But they did make you get up on the table and show them your special 'Monkey Dance' which was hilarious. *Then* everyone was laughing." Turbo made everyone laugh, and he'd played along like a great sport. He teased and joked and played pranks, but he could take it too.

Turbo shook his head. "Actually, I think everyone was laughing because I made you get up with me for the end, and that's when everyone realized half of your dress was missing."

"I was really angry about that." She had stewed about it for days. Even though it was a dress she'd picked up for a dollar at the secondhand store. It was the idea.

"Yeah. I have no idea why my brothers still tease me about the one woman who hates me," he said with more than a little sarcasm.

She crossed her arms over her chest. "You paid some old man to trade you places."

"That crafty old fellow made a hundred bucks off me." He shrugged. "I just wanted a dry place to sit." He lifted a hand and brushed a piece of her hair away from her face. She shivered at the light touch of his fingers.

"Then don't put spiders in my drink," she said softly.

He stepped closer, putting his arm around her. She stepped into his embrace, meeting him half-way.

His breath was shaky, and his voice low. "I guess we could have shared your chair. Then my brothers wouldn't have been teasing me for the last year about finding the woman who was not only immune to my supposedly amazing charms but who crawled under tables at wedding receptions to get away from me."

"So you have numerous charms?" Was she *flirting*? She was the serious librarian who *never* flirted.

"According to my brothers, I'm like Romeo on steroids."

"That's so? You've got all sorts of women under your spell?"

"I don't think so. The only woman I even remotely have wrapped around my finger is Miss Sally at the nursing home, and that's only because I ignore the fact that she licks her fingers while she's putting the cookies on the tray and I eat them anyway."

Harris shivered. "Better than cardboard?"

"Much. The oven bakes away the germs."

It wasn't the germs. It was the idea. But she didn't believe him about the girls. "I see. I seem to remember someone saying something about you walking in the front door with one woman and out the back with another."

"I don't know what you're talking about."

"Oh. So, you've never had a girlfriend?"

"I might have had a couple," he said with a sly grin that didn't confirm or deny his words.

"And you've never taken anyone else out and romanced them under the stars?" She tilted her head at what she hoped was a jaunty angle to hide how much she hoped he hadn't.

"No. I haven't done that before."

"And you've never kissed anyone?" She almost slapped a hand across her mouth. Where had that question come from?

"I'm not grilling you on your past." His voice stayed even, and he didn't seem upset.

She shrugged. "That's easy. I don't have one. You avoided the question."

"Never found any girl willing to let me practice."

"Oh, so you're looking for a practice girl so you can get prepared for the real woman?"

His eyes glinted. "Nope. Too late to start practicing."

"How so?"

"I found the one I want. Just don't know how the frig I'm going to talk her into taking me." His voice vibrated down into her chest.

Her heart pounded. He wouldn't be saying that, holding her close, if he had another girl he was interested in. It made her want to forget all the problems and just live. But it was only fair to warn him.

"I have to tell you something."

He closed his eyes and sighed. "I guess that means I have to tell you something too, but I don't really want to."

"Me either."

Chapter Fourteen

They stared at each other for a few long moments.

Harris swallowed. It was about time she took a chance in life. "What do you say we confess some other time and just practice kissing tonight?"

His eyes crinkled, and both sides of his mouth swung up. "I say..." He halted, and his eyes dimmed. "I say that you'll feel like I took advantage of you later." He leaned back, just a little.

"What if I promise not to?" She tilted her head. "You have to promise not to hate me either. And to not be too disappointed." She took a breath. "And to not ruin the play. Just act like we've never kissed at play practice."

Both of his rough hands came up and cupped her cheeks. "I could never hate you. I won't be disappointed, either." He froze. "Unless you're married?"

"No," she gasped in mock outrage, remembering her similar question of the night before.

"Okay. My secret doesn't involve anyone else, either."

"Mine either." Except the children she'd never have. "Not really."

"So, did we just decide we were going to live in the moment again?" he asked, his head leaning a little closer to hers.

"I think we did." She turned her head slightly and bit his thumb, which had nestled itself in the corner of her mouth.

His harsh exhale sent little pricks of power shooting up her spine. It felt good. Her lips turned up.

Turbo watched her reaction, his eyes lowered and heated. "Makes me think you have no idea how much control you have over me right now."

"Feels good," she whispered. "But I don't want to be powerful alone." She lowered her gaze. "You have the same over me."

He threaded his fingers through her hair. "Scary. I'm an idiot sometimes, and I don't want to hurt you."

His finger trembled as he traced her cheek, slow and gentle, as though she were precious china and he was afraid of breaking her.

Her heart skipped and scattered in her chest, and her limbs felt heavy. Her lips tingled.

"Don't hate me, Harris," he whispered, before his lips touched hers.

Light and dark exploded into glorious color. Her hands tightened into fists, gripping his t-shirt as her body leaned into him.

He feathered another kiss over her mouth as she strained upward. A little whimper escaped her when he pulled slightly away.

He growled, wrapping his arms around her and pulling her tight against him, his lips on hers, moving with urgency. The front of his grill dug into her back, but she barely noticed. Her hands slid up, shoving into his hair and dragging him closer still.

Her knees shook, her heart raced, and her world narrowed to Turbo, his taste and his scent, his touch and the sound of his harsh breathing.

He pulled back. She hissed in protest. He half-laughed, half-groaned as he closed his eyes. "If you want me to treat you like a lady, you'd better not make a sound like that again." He opened his eyes. "One kiss feels like a hundred more."

"A thousand more," she said, disappointment warring with red-hot desire spiraling through her body. Her blood rushed in her ears.

He took a deep breath before whispering, "Frig it," and lowering his head back down.

Long minutes later when he finally lifted his head, she was sitting on the hood of his pickup, with no memory of getting there, and he was pressed between her knees. He was panting. She, too, gasped for breath.

They stayed like that, staring at each other and breathing hard for what felt like eternity.

"As soon as I can walk without falling, I'm going to put you in your car."

She nodded.

Several more minutes went by as her breath and heart rate calmed.

Finally he put his hands on her waist and helped her off the hood of his truck.

"I hope I didn't dent it."

"Never thought I'd say I don't give a flip about my truck. Never saw anything better in my life than you sitting on it."

His strong arm wrapped around her waist as he walked her to her car and opened the door.

She wound the window down before shutting it.

He leaned down, his forearms resting on the top of the open window. "I know I'm going to be thinking about the last twenty minutes all freaking night. Wishing you were here."

His words warmed her chest. "Me too."

"You coming with me tomorrow?"

"Yeah." She couldn't remember where he was going, but at this point, she felt like she'd go anywhere he did.

"I'll pick you up. Seven too early?"

"I'll be ready."

He didn't move. Finally he said, "I hate that I'm not dropping you off at your door. Call me when you get home?"

"I'll text."

A shadow crossed his face. "Okay. Thanks. Be careful."

"I will."

She backed out slowly. Turbo, outlined by the porchlight behind him, stood with his legs braced and his arms hanging at his sides. It was all she could do to not put her car in drive and go back to him. But his desire to treat her with the respect he felt she deserved fortified her willpower, and she backed out onto the highway.

The drive home was a blur. Mostly because she couldn't get the thought of Turbo wanting kids out of her head. Maybe he wouldn't care. Maybe the neighborhood children would be enough. Maybe the idea of sitting on the couch, cozied up together, him reading a magazine, her a novel...or maybe they'd sit on a park bench in the fall and watch the leaves come down while taking turns reading poetry out loud. Books could take the place of kids. Turbo loved action and adventure, and there was no better place to find both than between the covers of a book.

She arrived at her home, greatly cheered by the thought, and texted Turbo to let him know she was safe and that she'd see him the next day. She almost added, I think I might be falling in love with you, but she deleted it. They could sort their feelings out some other time.

She had come to that conclusion and was about to drift off when Quincy texted her.

> I'm stuck on my story. Would you have time tomorrow to help? They haven't let me out of this prison yet.

Harris's heart caught. She wanted to help Turbo, but Quincy needed her more, she supposed. Plus, she knew what it was like to be stuck in the hospital with nothing to do.

> I'll be there. I'm off work until after noon. What time?

> I supposed they'll be done with their early morning bloodsucking by nine. You could come then?

> I'll be there.

> Bring Turbo. He makes my story funny.

> I'll try. He's trying to get his truck back together.

> Okay.

Harris bit her lip, before sucking it up and writing a long text to Turbo. Not fifteen seconds after she hit "send," her phone rang.

Turbo's number came up. She smiled. He was probably too impatient to text.

She pulled her covers up and cradled her phone. "Hello."

"Hey. What's up? Miss me already?"

"Didn't you read my text? Quincy wants help with her story tomorrow morning. She specifically asked for you too, but I told her you were working on your truck."

"Hmm." Turbo was silent for a moment. "What time?"

"She said by nine."

"Okay. That will work. I'll start on my hood a little earlier. I might have to beat Tough's butt out of bed. Seems like since he got married..." Turbo's voice trailed off. When he spoke again, it was lower and softer. "You make it to bed yet?"

It sent shivers down her spine, and she gripped the covers tighter, closing her eyes. "Yes. You?"

"Nah. Too keyed up."

"Sitting on the porch swing?" She could see him out there in the dark, pushing it slowly and dreaming up his next prank.

"Frig no. I'm here in the living room, working on my car."

"You know normal people do that in the garage."

"This house didn't come with one. So I'm making do."

"Your wife might have something to say about that."

"Ya think so? I hadn't really thought there'd ever be a woman who'd put up with me, but I've been running after one pretty hard lately. Maybe I'll let her catch me."

Harris laughed.

"Guess we'd have a hard time letting the kids play in the living room if I've got car parts all over it."

Her laugh caught in her throat. "You want kids?" she asked huskily.

"Yeah. At least ten. Been thinking lately I'm gonna put an order in for at least half of them to have red hair."

His words cracked her heart with a painful tear. Her throat closed, and she couldn't talk.

"Harris?" he said after she didn't say anything. But she couldn't stop the sniffle that came out. "You're crying. Rissy, girl. What did I do now?" His voice was low and soft and pleading.

She clenched her jaw. "Nothing. I can't have kids."

There were three beats of silence. She timed it.

"I'll be right there. Stay put."

She opened her mouth to protest, but he had already swiped off. Laying her phone beside her on her pillow, she brushed at the tears in her eyes. What was wrong with her? She'd known practically all her life that she'd not be able to have kids. Why was she crying?

But, of course, she knew. The idea that Turbo might be dreaming about having more, being more with her than what they were already. It made her heart sing. But the fact that he wanted ten kids...maybe he was joking about that many, but obviously they were important to him.

Still, she couldn't change the past, and she couldn't fix the future.

Cassidy had adopted. Harris had thought of that option and had it shot down by the first guy she mentioned it to.

The thing that she didn't think about much and really hated to face...the cancer could come back. Or, more likely, the treatments that had left her unable to have children could cause a different cancer to take her life. Early. Soon. And how fair would that be to a child who, for some reason, already had lost a mother? Not very.

She got out of bed, grabbing her robe, and slipped out of her room. She'd barely made it to her small kitchen before Turbo's pickup rumbled into her drive.

It jerked to a stop, and Turbo was out the door, jogging to her porch, before the motor quit completely. She opened the door, and he had his arms around her before she could open her mouth to tell him he didn't need to drive the whole way over. That she had been being a goose, and that she was fine. That she understood if he'd changed his mind about wanting red-haired children.

That thought made her eyes tear up again.

"Hey, Rissy. Honey. Please don't cry." His hands rubbed over her back before his arms tightened again. "I couldn't stand it when I was five miles away from you. Being here doesn't make it much easier. Man, it makes me feel so helpless when you cry. Please stop."

His whispered words and comforting touch only made the sobs rise up in her throat faster and harder until she was crying, loud and wet, into his shirt.

His hands stroked down her back and into her hair, until, finally, he put an arm under her knees and picked her up. Kicking her front door shut, he carried her to her couch where they'd watched *Annie*, and he sat, cradling her on his lap, kissing her forehead and cheeks, and murmuring sweet, loving words, begging her to stop crying.

Finally her sobs subsided into hiccups. His hands continued to stroke. His lips nuzzled her hair and wet cheeks.

Embarrassment made her chest tight. At least it was dark. She looked like a red-haired witch on dope when she cried like that. It had been a long time, too.

"I'm sorry," she whispered. "I didn't know I was going to act like that. I thought I'd accepted the fact that I couldn't have kids, but...I didn't realize how much I would long to..." She trailed off, unable to even put into words how much his words had made her want to have his baby.

"No. It's me. Just another example of my big, fat mouth getting me into trouble. Again. I didn't know you couldn't have kids, or I would never have said that."

"But you want kids."

His chest rose and fell, deeply. "I want you. However that looks."

"I had leukemia when I was in third grade."

He was quiet for a moment. "That's why I don't remember you in my class until I was in third grade. You missed a year of school..."

"And they held me back a grade. That's why I want this library for the kids so badly. If I had had a library in the hospital, maybe I would have been able to keep up on my schoolwork."

"This was your secret."

"Yes." She snuggled deeper, very aware that Turbo had tensed and still had not relaxed. Had he just now realized the implications? No children, ever? Could she ask? If she did, she risked hearing an answer that could devastate her.

"You know this doesn't matter to me." It was a statement. Flat-out serious.

The ball in her chest loosened slightly. "You just said how you wanted kids. Ten, actually."

"I want you. If that means no little babies with red hair, fine."

"We've never dated."

Again, he was uncharacteristically silent for a few minutes. "I guess you don't know I had the biggest crush on you in school."

She gasped. "What? Was that before or after you toilet papered my house, dumped a ton of shelled corn in my car, and glued my locker shut?"

"I was just trying to get your attention."

"You have a funny way of going about it."

"Yeah, I know."

"Oh, there was the paint you dumped on my head."

"That was actually an accident. But you did forget the prank call where I told you that you won the lottery?"

"That was you?"

"Yeah."

"Oh, wow. I never knew. You wouldn't believe it, but my grandmother had given me lottery tickets for Christmas. I didn't know how they worked, exactly. I mean, I didn't think you got a call about them, but I'd never had lottery tickets before."

"Yeah, I got you pretty good with that one."

"You did. I danced around the kitchen like a maniac. But you'd hung up, and I never found out how to get my money."

He laughed. "'Course, I fixed a flat tire for you once."

Her brows furrowed. He did?

"Yeah. I saw it on your car in the school parking lot. Pulled it off, put a plug in it during lunch. You never knew."

"No. I didn't."

He looked down, his face losing the ever-present smile and becoming serious. His voice came out soft and low, almost hesitant. "I've sent you flowers on the anniversary of your dad's death for the last fifteen years."

Harris's stomach dropped. Her hand went to cover her mouth, and her eyes filled with tears again. "Oh, wow." She swallowed, trying to get her throat to work. "I can't believe it. I never suspected."

"Figured you didn't, but I lost my mom five years before your dad died. I might miss my own birthday, but I'll never forget that date. January 19th. It's the worst day of the year."

"And you knew how I'd feel about my dad."

"Thought I might have an idea. 'Course, I was a kid and didn't have a very good imagination. Flowers seemed to be as good as anything."

"I've always wondered who that was...was that your secret?"

"Heck, no."

Chapter Fifteen

Turbo's heart jumped to his throat. She'd told hers. His turn.

He understood how she might think that not having kids might be a deal-breaker. Yeah, he loved kids, and more than that, he could admit his favorite daydream lately was having children with Harris. But Harris was the key to those dreams.

His secret, however, was so much worse. What woman wanted to end up shackled to a man who had the potential to embarrass her at any moment? Anytime someone handed him their phone and asked him to read a text, his wife would be sitting there with her heart in her throat wondering if that person was going to find out that her husband was stupid. Harris deserved so much more.

His pride couldn't take Harris thinking he was stupid. How could he take that chance?

"Rissy?" He'd called her that earlier, and she hadn't seemed to mind. He liked the idea of him having a special name for her. Let everyone else see her as the prim librarian who was quiet and studious. He'd kissed her. He knew there was a passion that ran deep. But it was perfectly okay with him if the rest of the world never found out about it. They could use her full name and think she was exactly what she seemed.

"Yeah?"

"Is it okay if I call you Rissy?"

"I like it, actually. I've never had a nickname."

He laughed. "I like the idea of having something just between us."

"Me too." Her fingers tickled the hair at the nape of his neck, and he tried not to move. He didn't want her to stop, but he probably should think about putting her back to bed and going home. He'd be fine in the morning, but she'd be tired.

"Turbo?"

"Hmm?"

"I don't have any more secrets."

Oh, crap. He didn't want to ruin anything. Plus, she'd just cried her heart out. It was too soon to drop another bomb on her. "Can I tell you mine tomorrow? After the play rehearsal." There. He'd set a deadline for himself. A possible end date for their relationship.

She snuggled deeper into his arms. "That's fine."

He tightened his hold, feeling guilty for putting it off. For even stealing this time with her.

"Thanks for coming."

"I couldn't stay at home while you were here, crying." He gazed down at her, and she smiled a watery smile back at him.

"It made me feel like you really cared."

"Guess that cat's out of the bag."

She laughed.

He cupped her cheek with the hand that wasn't under her back. "I care. A lot." He swallowed, unused to talking about his feelings but wanting her to know. "I've never raced across town in the middle of the night because my heart wouldn't let me do anything else."

"Your heart?"

"I've got one. Surprised?"

"No. I'm surprised it was for me."

"Only you."

TURBO DIDN'T GET in until three. He was up again at five to go after his hood. Harris hadn't said she'd still come, and he wasn't planning on getting her. He figured he'd get his hood, stick it on, and be back to pick her up by nineish, and they'd head into the hospital together.

He snorted. Because, for the first time in his life, hanging out at the library seemed like a great idea.

The lights were on in Tough's garage when Turbo pulled in, pulling his trailer behind. He'd texted Tough last night around two a.m., but he hadn't expected Tough to be here.

Nor the old men who hung out at Tough's garage, like the quilting club at Torque's. But when he opened the door, he was met by two grumpy old men arguing over who got to be the black checkers.

"I was here six minutes before you."

"But I sat down here first."

"Because someone had to make the coffee. That was obviously me, since your coffee tastes worse than railroad cinders."

"What do you know about railroad cinders? You were just a whippersnapper when they came out with the diesel motors."

"I not only rode on the old steam engines, I shoved coal into the firebox. It was my first job. I was six years old. Unlike you, who laid around the house until your mother kicked you out."

"That's not true. I started my first business when I was ten. That was before you were born."

Turbo punched the button on the overhead door, and it started up. Both men turned from the checkerboard where they were standing. Tough looked up from where he was pouring coffee. He held a cup up.

Mr. Sigel said, "No. Don't give that stuff to Turbo. Last time you did that, he was literally hanging from the ceiling."

Turbo rolled his eyes. "I was on the ceiling because my magic trick went a little awry and Tough didn't want the Borax mixture that exploded and landed on the light to get hot. It wasn't the coffee."

"It was the coffee."

The men nodded together.

Turbo opened his mouth.

Tough had come over beside him. "Shut up. First time since two o' clock yesterday afternoon that they're actually agreeing on something."

Turbo closed his mouth. He whispered, "It wasn't the coffee."

"It was too," Al said from across the garage.

"How come when I talk to you, you never hear me, but when I'm saying something I don't want you to hear, you hear it every time?"

"Huh?" Al said.

"Like that," Turbo said.

Tough grinned and shook his head.

"Where's Kelly?"

"Sleeping." Tough shifted. "She needs it."

Turbo laughed. "Why? She's grumpy if she doesn't get enough rest?" He'd never had that problem, thankfully. Lack of sleep just made him hyper. Everything made him hyper. It hadn't bothered him until Harris. Would she put up with how screwed up he was?

"Nah. She's about three months along and needs the extra rest."

"Three months along...you're gonna have a baby?"

"No. She is."

Turbo punched Tough on the shoulder. "That's what I meant. Congratulations. I'm happy for you." A small shot of envy zipped through him. He'd never considered how some people had children easily and others...didn't. His heart ached for Harris.

Tough pointed to the hood. "Back your trailer in, and I'll use the skid loader to lift it on."

"Make sure he doesn't park over the white line. Screws with my hearing aid when you've got something there. I get some kind of rap station playing on it."

"He said that the last time I was here. Is that true?" Turbo asked Tough under his breath.

"Darn straight it's true, you little whelp," Al called from across the garage. "Ya think I'm a liar?"

"No, of course not."

Tough shrugged. "Just watch the line. True or not, it's not worth listening to the complaining."

After hopping back in his pickup and backing the trailer up, stopping on the right side of the white line, Tough loaded the hood up. They strapped it down, while the old men argued about a technical detail in the checkers rulebook.

"How's the play practice coming?" Tough asked.

Turbo had to hand it to him; he only smirked a little.

"Not bad."

"I'm sorry we pushed you into it, but of anyone I know, you're the biggest ham. You probably should have been an actor. If it weren't for your ugly mug..." Tough pointed around his face.

"Oh, please. I just didn't want to have to go around fake kissing women I don't like." Turbo was totally joking. He had trucks in his blood. He'd never leave his rig for Hollywood.

"Yeah, so how's that kissing part going on the play?"

"Haven't had to do it yet."

Mr. Sigel had shuffled over. "Enjoy it while you can."

"You gotta stick with one girl, Turbo. Don't listen to this old coot," Al said with a nod at Mr. Sigel.

"Yeah, I'm the one-girl type. Just have to find a girl I'm good enough for," Turbo mumbled. If only.

"What about that little redhead you were running around with?" Mr. Sigel asked before jumping one of Al's black checkers.

"How'd you know I was running around with anyone?" Turbo countered.

Tough shoved his hands in his pockets. "They gossip every day with the quilting club. It's almost a competition as to who knows what first."

"Do they know Kelly's pregnant?" Mr. Sigel asked.

Tough rolled his eyes and shook his head. "See?"

"We'll have to make a trip down there later." Mr. Sigel said.

Turbo grinned and waved. "I'm headed there now. I'll probably forget and tell them myself."

"Hey, wait a second, I'll ride along." Mr. Sigel grabbed his cane and hobbled toward the passenger side door.

"Think I'll go too." Al was a little more spry and made it to the front door first.

"Hey. I called it. You ride in the back."

"I'm here first. Make me."

Turbo grinned. "What are they doing up so early anyway?"

"They have a sixth sense about these things. Always seem to know when something's going down."

"I see." Turbo turned in time to see Harris's small car pulling up outside the garage along the sidewalk. His heart started hitting in his chest like the pistons in a hot engine. He didn't even finish his conversation with Tough but moved out, his eyes on the red-haired woman who was stepping from her car.

"Good morning." She pushed her hair back and smiled up at him. So beautiful she made his eyes hurt.

"It just got better."

Her smile widened. "You never said anything about picking me up, and you didn't answer my text, so I came here."

He patted his pants' pocket. "Phone's in the cab."

She tilted her head. "Is it okay that I'm here?"

"I wanted to let you sleep, but I'd rather have you with me." He opened the driver's side door of his truck and stuck his head in. "My girl's riding in the front."

"They can drive my car over if they want," Harris said.

"Can't. Ungrateful kids took my license."

"Bunch of spoiled bums," Al said. "When I hear my kids are coming, I hide mine in a cup of water in the freezer. They haven't found it yet. I'll drive." He patted Mr. Sigel's shoulder. "You can ride with me. Kids don't appreciate nothing anymore."

"You got that right." The old men put their arms around each other's shoulders and shuffled toward Harris's car. "Let's get out of here. If we leave first, we'll be able to break the news about Tough's baby to the quilters ourselves." They cackled together before creaking slowly into Harris's car.

Harris's eyes slammed back to him. "Kelly's pregnant?"

Turbo shrugged. "Guess so."

Harris stared at him. "Why didn't you tell me? Why didn't *she* tell me?" She looked past him to Tough. "Why didn't *you* tell me?" Then she rolled her eyes. "Never mind." Tough didn't talk much.

Turbo held his hands up at Harris's accusatory tone. "I just found out. Like minutes ago."

Tough had walked back over to the coffee counter. "Want some joe?"

"Not him," one of the old men called from outside the garage. They had to be indicating Turbo.

Turbo grinned at Harris. "You want someone else besides Joe?"

"Maybe." She lifted her head, and he didn't hesitate, kissing her sweetly and a little long.

He broke the kiss off with them both a little breathless and, putting a hand around her waist, threw a hand up at Tough. "See you later. Thanks for the hood."

"I'll send you a bill."

"Ha. It's been paid."

"Guess we'll see if you actually show up on opening night." Tough smirked. He stretched. "It's early, and the old men are gone. I'm going back to bed for a while."

"I notice you didn't say back to sleep."

Tough just grinned and walked into his office. His small apartment connected to the other side.

Harris's body had stiffened, and Turbo thought back. "I'm showing up."

"I know."

He took a hold of her shoulders. "No. I'm really showing up."

She cupped his face with her hand. "I know you are."

It didn't take long to drive to Torque's. Harris jumped out and ran into the garage, opening the overhead door so Turbo could back his trailer in, parking in front of the truck.

It was barely seven a.m., but the quilting club was already seated at their chairs, with Mr. Sigel and Al busy whispering as the ladies' needles flew in and out.

"She hasn't killed you yet?" Beulah called to Turbo.

"Nope. Not yet." Turbo grinned as he put his arm around Harris.

"She's letting you awful close. Girl, has that guy given you a ring yet?"

Harris laughed and shook her head, but Turbo noted her bright red cheeks.

"Make him treat you right, girl," Miss Betty said with a lowered-brow look at Turbo.

"He is."

Turbo thought of last night. He'd not wanted to leave. But he had, and he was glad now for it. He didn't want Harris to have to defend him. Or to have anyone think less of her because of him.

Which made him stop. Could he learn to read? People would always be thinking less of Harris because of him unless he overcame this issue that lay like a lead cover over his head. He'd tried in school. Up until about fourth grade. Then he'd quit, more focused on cheating the system that had left him behind.

Could he do it now? He shoved the thought aside to think about later. When he was alone.

"Hey. I forgot. I have something to show you ladies." He looked down at Harris and winked. "Hold on," he said low.

Moving away from her, he walked over to his rig and opened the dog box. "Remember those quilting squares you ladies gave me. Then, very unhelpfully, told me that I'd never learn to quilt?"

"How could we forget? You said quilting wasn't nowhere near as hard as we tried to make it."

"Well, look at this." He pulled the nine-square he'd made out of the bag where he'd stashed it and held it up.

The ladies' eyes squinted, but Al and Mr. Sigel guffawed. "Guess he showed you. Nice job, Turbo. I never took you for a quilter."

Turbo allowed an arrogant smile to lift the corners of his mouth. "You all can apologize to me right about now."

"Hold on just one cotton-picking minute. Bring that thing a little closer here." Miss Alda lowered her glasses and studied his "quilt" as he obediently walked closer. "Don't stop. Get on over here. Right now. Stop here." She thrust her sewing needle toward the floor right in front of her feet. Knowing he was busted, Turbo inched to the spot before handing his "quilt" over into her outstretched hand.

She studied it, turning it over in her hands.

"What kind of stitches does he have?" Miss Angelina asked. "They big, preschool type stitches?"

"I don't see any stitches," Miss Alda said, shoving her glasses back on her face and lowering her head to look closer.

Miss Beulah leaned over her shoulder, adjusting her own glasses.

"Okay, ladies, that's enough." Turbo reached for his quilt.

"Not so fast." Miss Alda yanked it back. Rather quickly for an eighty-year-old woman, Turbo thought.

Miss Betty leaned closer. "There are no stitches."

"You're right!" Miss Alda exclaimed. "What did he..." She pulled at the material.

"You glued it," Miss Angelina said with a giggle. "He glued it. Of course he did. My brilliant boy." She toddled over and patted Turbo on the shoulder, since she couldn't reach the top of his head, probably. "You glued it. You always figure everything out."

"And that's why I love you," Turbo said, hugging her considerable girth. "You always think the best of me."

"I say that's cheating," Miss Beulah said.

"I say it's pure genius," Mr. Sigel said. He looked at Turbo. "How long did it take you?"

"Couple minutes. Maybe thirty." Turbo grinned.

"Yeah, like I said, pure genius. These old biddies spend hours and hours trying to get the same effect. And you had it done in thirty minutes. Brilliant, I say."

"But what about when he washes it?" Miss Alda asked. "Will it fall apart?"

"It's probably toxic. I wouldn't want my baby anywhere near that," Miss Alda declared.

"You never had any babies."

"If I had, Miss Particular, I wouldn't have wanted them anywhere near something toxic like that. I bet you can't even put that in a landfill. You probably have to have someone come and cart it away. Put it in the same place they haul needles and blood and radioactive stuff."

"Don't be ridiculous," Miss Betty said. "It's just glue." She eyed Turbo. "Is it waterproof?"

"Yes. And nontoxic. I checked."

"He might be on to something, ladies," Miss Beulah said with a thoughtful look.

There was a general murmur of disapproval. "But I like quilting. I don't want to glue."

"No. You're just afraid of change. If something better comes along, it's okay to be off with the old and on with the new," Miss Beulah said with confidence.

"Unless it's another man. Then you're stuck with the same old same old." Miss Betty pushed her glasses up on her nose, hiding her smirk.

"Unless you have a man like mine. He was totally okay with the whole off with the old, which just so happened to be me." Angelina's droopy eyes still pinched with a hint of the old pain.

"You're sounding a little bitter. Glad I never got married. I had a nice, full life and didn't need a man to complete me." Miss Alda straightened in her chair and resumed her stitching.

"Okay," Turbo interrupted. "Nice to see you ladies, but Harris and I have to be moving on." He turned toward Harris, who had been watching the goings-on with interest. "Don't let them convince you that you don't need a man."

"Well, I have been getting on pretty good without one."

"That's in the past."

She took his hand. "I'm open to new ideas."

They smiled at each other, bidding the elderly folks goodbye, and headed back to Turbo's truck where Torque had unhooked the trailer.

"You need me?" Turbo asked his brother.

"Nah. Did I hear you were planning to visit the hospital?"

"Yeah, I have a book to help write."

"Oh, you're going to be a millionaire. That's great. I'll put the hood on, you give me a cut of the proceeds."

"Hardly." Turbo laughed. He couldn't help it. After all, he was headed out to help write a book, and he couldn't even really read. How funny was that? Harris gave him a quizzical look but allowed him to take her hand and lead her to his truck.

"You guys can go ahead and drive back over to Tough's. I'll be there to pick up Harris's car at some point."

They got in his pickup and headed toward the hospital.

Chapter Sixteen

hings were quiet and slow at the pediatric cancer ward.

A few little boys played with trucks on the floor, while a couple of little girls in soft pajama pants sat around a dollhouse. Several teens, their IV lines hovering close by, sat on chairs around the periphery.

Quincy had her notebook out and her legs stretched out over the cushion of the one loveseat in the room.

Harris felt a little conspicuous walking in with Turbo's arm slung possessively over her shoulders. A couple of nurses lifted eyebrows, and one smiled, but no one said anything. She was thankful. She had thought of herself as not dating, not girlfriend material, never getting married for so long, she needed time to adjust to the fact that Turbo was okay with her, just the way she was. Seemed to still like her.

Like the fact that he even noticed or liked her in the first place wasn't shocking enough. After all, if there was a modern equivalent of a wallflower, it was her.

That wasn't to say she wasn't enjoying it, because she was. Last night was the first time in her memory that someone had held her while she cried.

Not that she blamed her mother. Having a young daughter being diagnosed with leukemia would be devastating, then to have your husband die on top of that, leaving you with one very sick child and two more very young children...well, her mother did the best she could. And Harris had spent a lot of time alone in the hospital, reading the backs of shampoo bottles.

She always talked to her mother on Sunday afternoons. She'd have to remember to tell her who had sent her flowers on the anniversary of her dad's death. They'd wondered about that together through the years.

She pressed close to Turbo, and his arm automatically tightened. He looked down, questions in his eyes. Giving him a reassuring smile, she nodded to Quincy and slipped out from under his arm to walk over, feeling the coolness of the air and realizing that she'd been missing something special.

"How's your story going?" she asked Quincy who jerked, as though she'd been deep in thought. "Sorry. Hope you didn't lose your train of thought."

"No. I was just trying to figure out how to write this without it being so blatantly obvious."

"What's obvious?"

"That being sick sucks."

"Well, it does."

Quincy's lips flattened, and she looked away, her shoulders set. "How would you know?"

"I lived in Iowa when I had leukemia, so I wasn't in this hospital, but..."

"You had leukemia?"

"Yes."

"You survived."

She ran her hands up and down, indicating her body. "I'm here."

"Did it...did it ever come back?"

"No. They said I'm cured." It was always there, in the back of her mind, a constant little whisper—if she sneezed, if she felt tired, if she had a pain anywhere—was that cancer? She'd looked up the stats. She knew the odds. But she'd learned to shove the little voice aside. For the most part.

Quincy thought on that for a while. Then she held up her notebook. "Any ideas?"

Harris gave an internal chuckle at the fickleness of the teen mind. She remembered it all too well.

"Why don't you tell it from the perspective of a truck?" Turbo's voice came from the floor where he and the little boys had their trucks lined up. Motor noises filled the large playroom.

"That would work if you wanted it to be for children." Harris tapped her chin. "Maybe Elsie would draw pictures for your story."

Quincy's eyes brightened, and she looked over to where Elsie, another teenager, sat at the window. She spoke in a low tone. "She's not doing so hot. The docs gave her a bad report. I guess a project like this would take her mind off it if she decides to do it."

"You know, I can look into this, but I've had a lot of self-published authors coming into the library with actual physical books. They're getting them printed somewhere. I could see if maybe printing a few copies would be an option. We'd include it in our new library, of course." Harris nodded in the direction of the empty rooms, still waiting to be filled with books, which were going to be the library.

"Really? You really think we could publish it?"

"Sure. And I think Turbo's right. If you write it from the perspective of a truck...maybe one that is broken down and has to go to the shop. That, obviously, would represent being sick."

"Don't forget the driver, though. He has to be handsome, strong, and brave," Turbo interjected from his spot on the floor.

"And humble," Harris added.

"And the sidekick has to have red hair."

"I think the hero should actually be a heroine, and she should have red hair, and the sidekick can have laughing brown eyes."

Turbo's grin split wide open. "You like my eyes, huh?"

"I don't think I said that." Harris looked to Quincy for confirmation.

Quincy shook her head. "That's definitely NOT what you said. But we're not going to argue about it. I need to think."

"You can give the truck human emotions. But it can do truck things.

Like, instead of having an IV, it could need air in the tires, and instead of surgery, it could have all its parts lying around."

Quincy nodded.

Harris added, "I can bring in some children's books, but a lot of times the pictures say as much as the words. I think Elsie would do a fabulous job. I've seen her work, and she's really good." She tapped her chin again. "But she might not have any idea what the inside of a truck looks like." She looked over at Turbo. "Do you have any pictures?"

"Are you kidding?" He sat up, pulling his phone from his pocket. "I have more pictures of my truck than most people have of their children. Someday..." He stopped abruptly, and his eyes, full of concern, snapped up to Harris.

She shook her head and lifted a shoulder, but her heart squeezed painfully. He'd be such a good dad.

He showed them some of the pictures of his motor being torn down along with other pics and ideas.

"We need to talk to Elsie," Quincy said.

"May I have this for a few minutes?" Harris held up Turbo's phone.

"Sure." He never hesitated. His easy agreement made her feel good. Obviously there wasn't anything on there that he was worried about her, or young teens, seeing. Just that thought deepened her respect for him even more. But she couldn't forget the look in his eyes when he talked about the pictures and his kids.

It didn't take much convincing to talk Elsie into being willing to try her hand at drawing a few pictures for a story. After some more discussion, with Turbo piping in with ideas, they cleaned up the toys on the floor. The kids begged for a magic trick before they left, and Turbo made one ball turn into five. As closely as Harris watched, she couldn't figure out how he did it.

They said goodbye, promised to stay in touch with Elsie and Quincy, and left the hospital.

"Let me buy you lunch?" Turbo asked on the way out, his arm once again draped over her shoulders.

He stopped at a diner where they were served quickly. By the time Turbo pulled into Tough's where her car was sitting, it was time for Harris to get going.

"I'll see you at practice tonight?" she said to Turbo as he opened her car door.

"I'll be there."

Could she ask him if he would pay attention and be helpful or if he planned to be disruptive and a distraction like again? She couldn't get her mouth to form the words. She wanted to believe he had put all that behind him. After their last kiss, after the possessive way he'd held her today, surely he was on her side with the play.

"I'm planning on doing a run-though with actions onstage and not just a sit and read. There's also music practices tonight and tomorrow."

"I'm ready." He adjusted his ball cap, his dark brown hair curling out from under the sides.

Her fingers itched to touch it, but she gripped her door handle and slipped into her car. Something she hadn't mentioned and didn't plan on discussing was the fact that there was a kiss between Daddy Warbucks and Grace. It had been a nonissue so far since they'd only done a few read-throughs yesterday. Tonight, she would have to watch Turbo get romantic with another woman. For pretend.

People did it all the time.

Problem was, she didn't do it all the time. She'd never had a serious boyfriend before, if that's what her relationship with Turbo even was. Watching him onstage tonight was going to be hard; she couldn't deny it. But she wanted him to be serious, too. Her whole chest felt like a battle was raging inside, and she didn't know what to do or how to act. She was used to her life being calm and predictable and not this crazy, emotional combat in her mind.

Turbo closed her door. He leaned down on her open window. "Thanks for spending your time off with me."

"I enjoy being with you." Harris studied her hands; her fingers picked at the steering wheel. "But..."

She looked over at Turbo, caught him as the laughter faded from his eyes, replaced with a wariness she hated because it came because of her.

The very stillness of his body showed his unease.

She swallowed. Hard. "I'm not sure I can do...us...tonight." She breathed out and glanced at his face.

He flinched. Almost imperceptibly. His eyes were flat brown. He nodded. "I understand."

"I'm not sure you do."

He straightened, his eyes now completely shaded by the brim of his cap. "No, I do. I get it. You'll come to my house at night and kiss me until I'd do anything you want me to, then at play practice, you want to pretend to barely know me because if anyone knew that the straight-laced librarian was slowly seducing this dumb truck driver, your stress level would be uncontrollable." A muscle jumped in his jaw. He looked down the street.

"That's not quite it."

"You can't say I'm wrong. You're not exactly proud to be showing me off to your friends. Whatever it is that you feel for me isn't something you want, it's something you fight." His jaw muscle popped in and out. "I'm not an asset. I'm a liability. And you don't want to deal with that tonight. I told you. I get it." He slapped the roof of her car and backed away. "Don't worry. I won't upset you by insisting we need to do 'us' tonight. And if you show up at my house afterward and want to kiss me senseless, I'm not so proud that I'd turn you away." He turned and walked toward the garage.

"Turbo, wait." A quick glance at her dash showed that she had barely enough time to drive across town to make it to work on time, but her chest ached and she couldn't breathe. She'd hurt Turbo. Right in the spot where he was vulnerable, and she hadn't even realized it. But what could she do? She didn't have enough time to backtrack.

He stopped but didn't turn around. He lifted his ball cap and ran a hand through his overlong hair before shoving it back down on his head. His hands dropped, and he stood still with his back toward her.

Her heart beat fast, and her neck felt cold then hot. She couldn't find the words to tell him how he was wrong. Did that mean he was right? Was she really just a snob who was ashamed of the first man who'd ever shown any interest in her?

She wasn't ashamed of Turbo. Was she? It was more about him disrupting the practice, and if he did that and everyone knew they were seeing each other too... And yeah, there'd be some surprise that she'd have to deal with on top of everything else.

"We'll have to talk about this later. I need to get to work."

He didn't say anything but started walking again.

Harris gritted her teeth before yanking her seatbelt out and slamming it in the buckle. After she turned around, she couldn't resist a look in her rearview mirror. Turbo stood with his hands braced against the side of the garage, his head down.

He looked so dejected and discouraged that her heart cracked. Another glance at the time showed she had no choice but to keep going, as much as she wanted to turn around and make him believe she wasn't ashamed of him or their relationship. As confident and cocky as he always seemed, it was almost inconceivable to her that innocent words she hadn't meant to come out in a mean-spirited way had hurt him so badly.

At the next stoplight, she texted him. It was a long enough wait that she was able to get in about six sentences explaining that he'd misunderstood.

After she hit "send," the light was still red. She scrolled up. He'd never texted her. How had she not noticed that before?

He hadn't answered by the time the light turned green. She made it to the library parking lot with two minutes to spare.

Digging her keys out of her purse on her way up the library steps, Harris knew she wouldn't have time to breathe until after practice was over tonight, since the library was hosting a book club this afternoon, movie night for elementary kids after school, and pizza and a book night for teens until closing. Not to mention their back rooms were always booked up in the fall.

She took one last look at her blank phone before shoving it in her purse. She'd see Turbo tonight and explain.

Chapter Seventeen

Turbo walked into the old theater at seven thirty on the dot. He'd already spent two hours practicing the music with the music director and the small orchestra of volunteers they'd put together. The songs hadn't been hard to learn, and he'd done okay with his parts, even if he couldn't read a lick of the music or words that they'd handed him to use.

He'd been able to be funny and personable, as everyone expected him to be, and no one had known that his chest felt empty. How something that felt empty could also be on fire was a mystery he'd maybe try to figure out another time. He didn't have the heart for it today.

He'd stopped at the restroom before leaving and allowed everyone else to get out ahead of him. Because the scenery people were working on the stage, they'd practiced in the church next door. Handy that the music director of the church was also the one directing the music for the play.

That's how everyone else was in their place, with Harris standing on the stage, explaining what was going to happen.

Her long hair was caught up in a bun, which emphasized her slender white neck and high cheekbones.

His heart pinched. Okay, so his chest wasn't completely empty. It could still feel pain.

Removing his ball cap, he shoved his other hand in his pocket and slid in the last row, throwing his hat down on the seat beside him. He'd quit early and showered, dressed as he always had in a button-down shirt and clean jeans, good boots. His hair was dry, but he'd noticed it was curling at the ends, and he needed a cut. Not for the first time in his life, he wished for a pair of dog clippers. Sitting still in the barber's chair was torture.

Harris's voice washed over him. How could these other people sit here and listen to her and not break out in goosebumps? Slightly husky, totally seductive, her voice had captivated him long ago. No wonder she was able to get little kids to sit still and listen to her read. Even at their young ages, they could tell there was something magical about her voice.

Her eyes skipped over him. His fingers tightened on the armrest. Yeah, he'd figured she wouldn't want to be talking to him here. He shoved down the burning in the back of his throat.

She continued to talk, saying they'd go through the whole thing, hoping that many had their lines memorized. He grimaced. He'd had an earbud in all afternoon and *Annie* playing constantly.

Harris reminded them how soon it was until the first production. She also mentioned that she'd had a report about online sales from the theater, and they'd been stronger than she'd expected.

"We're twenty tickets from selling out." She took a deep breath. "I'd like to add two matinees, Saturday afternoon and Sunday afternoon. I'd also like to consider opening up the dress rehearsal Friday night to paid attendees. Maybe at a discount."

There was some discussion about it, and they decided to give it a go. It didn't matter to Turbo. So he stayed out of the discussion. He'd just have to make sure he got home in time on Friday afternoon, since his truck was finally done and ready to roll. He hoped he didn't get caught in traffic anywhere on Friday, either, that would make him last for their dress rehearsal.

The rehearsal started. Many of the actors were still holding their scripts. Camila didn't. Mia didn't either. She was a true professional. And she was doing a great job. According to the movie, he was supposed to kiss her tonight. He didn't have a clue what the play version actually said. He'd considered asking, since the subject hadn't been broached in their read-throughs, either.

As Turbo watched, he was impressed with the local high school's drama department, which was taking care of all the sound effects, special effects, and scenery changes. He hadn't expected it to be this good.

He went over several of the tricky parts in his head—the ones that didn't follow the movie. That's where he always got stuck and where Harris thought he was deliberately goofing. Well, he wasn't going to deliberately goof today. He wasn't sure, exactly, what he actually was going to do, but...something. He was going to do something, if he couldn't remember his lines.

He didn't worry about it; he'd faked it so many times before, something would occur to him if he needed it. So he was able to get into the performance.

Acting was fun, and he enjoyed it. He supposed his brothers were right, he was a natural ham. It was easy to smile and be benevolent to Camila. A little harder to put any kind of heat in his gaze for Grace, as they undressed Annie together after the movie. Punjab and Miss Hannigan did their parts amazingly well, and they pulled him up.

He stumbled a couple of times with his lines, but since he wasn't holding his book, Harris called them out to him, and he didn't have to find an excuse for not reading. All in all, it went well until they came to the scene that replaced the helicopter scene. They had changed it to a car scene, where Punjab was with him and they were searching for Annie. He'd fumbled this many times, especially since the dialogue was so different than the movie and it was only Punjab and him, so he had to carry half the conversation. He adlibbed a lot, which annoyed Harris. Finally she cut the scene for the fourth time. She walked onstage and handed him her script.

"Here. Just read this, then go home tonight and study. You have everything else down so well, it's a mystery as to why this part gives you fits." She paused, and he read the little bit of fear in her eyes before she covered it. "I can stay after tonight if you want to work on this part."

"I could help too," Mia called from backstage.

Harris's eyes flickered. Her chin jutted out. "Just start right here, at the second line." She pointed her finger to somewhere on the page.

Turbo's breath came fast, and his heart pounded in his ears. He couldn't do the goof-off stuff he usually did. She was tired of it, and she took it like he was disrespecting her every time. With the sound people and the scenery people and the stagehands, plus the entire cast…there were even more people here today, and she would feel even more disrespected and embarrassed if he made everyone laugh and somehow weaseled out of reading this. Again.

In his mind, it suddenly became very clear. He could fudge, wiggle, make everyone laugh, and somehow get someone else to read him his lines, which would embarrass and annoy Harris. Or he could admit the truth. Which would embarrass no one but himself and would make no one but himself look bad. If he did it now, before anyone knew that Harris and he might have been a couple, she wouldn't even have to deal with that added issue, and he would never embarrass her again.

Her jaw tightened, and her eyes narrowed. She pointed at the spot on the page again. "Are you going to start?"

Her gaze asked, *Or are you going to start your stupid crap that makes the entire cast think this is a comedy show?*

He stood from the chair that doubled as his seat in the car.

"I can't."

Her head jerked back, and she blinked. "You can't?" Immediately, her eyes narrowed. "Would you care to explain why you can't, Mr. Baxter?"

He took a deep breath. His temple pounded, and blood rushed in his ears. His vision narrowed so the only thing he saw was Harris. "I would if I could. But I have no idea where you want me to start or what I'm supposed to say, because I can't read." He let out a shaky breath and tried and failed to gather enough spit to swallow.

Harris stood still. Her mouth opened and closed.

Dimly, Turbo registered a few titters behind him, like someone thought he was joking. He didn't move, and of course, he didn't laugh, and the titters subsided into stunned silence.

~

EVERY INTERACTION she'd had with Turbo replayed through Harris's mind in the short seconds that ticked by. His refusal to help with the scripts, his threat to deliver the wrong library books to the nursing home residents, how he talked her into watching the movie instead of studying the lines, how he'd helped with the book—but only by giving ideas, not by writing anything down—how he'd never texted her...but mostly how he'd made a joke anytime he didn't know his lines at all the practices they'd had so far. He joked to take the focus off the fact that he couldn't read. And he'd just taken that focus and admitted something humbling and shameful to keep her from feeling disrespected and like she was losing control of the practice. Because he'd promised he wouldn't do it anymore.

He'd kept his word.

And he couldn't read. It was true. She knew it with all her heart. This wasn't another of his goofy jokes or pranks.

She didn't know what to say.

She didn't know what to do, either. Her heart had swelled so big and so thick in her chest that it felt like it would burst.

Suddenly the quiet that had descended on the entire stage burst into excited talking. People pointed to the door, but Harris couldn't look. Her gaze was held captive by Turbo's.

"Why didn't you tell me?" she asked softly. Then she realized. It was his secret. This, *this*, was what he knew would be a deal-breaker between them. She shook her head. Was it? "You can't read at all?"

One side of his mouth tightened. His jaw twitched. But he answered. "A few small words. My name. I can write my address."

He looked vulnerable in a way she'd never seen before. Her heart melted. It couldn't change anything. He was still the same man who cared for kids and who hung out at the nursing home and who helped a little girl with cancer write a book and who used his truck as entertainment for the sick. Still the same man who cut and split firewood for the elderly and held her under the stars and kissed her with an explosive passion she'd never felt before.

But he couldn't *read*.

She was a *librarian*.

"Hey, Harris! Look who just walked back in," someone yelled.

Turbo's face was expressionless. He wasn't begging her to understand or even accept. It was like he was okay with however she reacted. She just didn't know how to react. She was so...shocked. How had he fooled everyone all his life? How had he even graduated? She was there. She saw him graduate. The principal had handed him a diploma.

"Harris?"

She jerked her gaze away from Turbo's deep brown eyes.

"Yeah?" She cleared her throat, hoping her voice dropped back into its normal octave, since that last word sounded like Minnie Mouse had taken up residence in her throat. It wouldn't have surprised her.

Turbo couldn't read.

"What?" she asked Camila, who was tugging on her arm.

"Look." She pointed at the foot of the stage. "Daddy Warbucks is back."

"Ransom Blythe?" Harris walked over, squinting. "Is that you?" He was supposed to be playing off-Broadway. But her ex-Daddy Warbucks was, indeed, back.

He smiled, confident and a little cocky. "It is. I figured I'd come back and see if you still want me."

"But I thought you were doing an..."

"Didn't pan out," he said before she could finish. He shrugged. "I don't have anything else going on and figured I'd come on back and see if you still wanted me." It was phrased as a pleasant conversation, but his tone indicated he expected to be given the part.

"Well..." She straightened.

Turbo had shoved both hands in his pockets and walked around the "car." He stopped a good ten feet away from her. She could read nothing in his expression.

How could she tell Ransom she didn't need him? After all, Turbo was doing better than she'd ever thought he would. But this man was a professional, and she had to be careful of his ego.

While she was still trying to form the words, Turbo spoke. "I'll save you the trouble of figuring things out, Harris." He paused. "I quit."

Harris wouldn't have been more surprised if he'd turned into a zebra and announced he was running for president. It took her several seconds to stop her mouth from opening and closing. It was the second time in the last ten minutes that he'd shocked her.

Before she could gather her wits, he'd strode off the stage, his stride confident, the tilt of his broad shoulders just as cocky as ever.

She opened her mouth to call after him.

Ransom jumped onto the stage. "Well, that settles it, then. I spent the ride back from NYC reviewing my lines. I already had them memorized, and I'm ready to jump in." He kept talking about the car and the scene. Harris heard him, but her eyes followed Turbo as he walked out the back doors of the theater. He didn't turn around.

Chapter Eighteen

Thursday evening, Turbo bobtailed into his driveway. He'd dropped his trailer at Torque's and planned to do the brakes on it the next day, since the load he had been scheduled to pick up this evening had cancelled.

Just as well. He'd run almost nonstop all week, starting Sunday afternoon. After his truck had been down, he needed the income to catch himself back up.

If his load for tonight hadn't cancelled on such short notice, he would have searched harder for a replacement. After all, the idea of slowing down or, heaven forbid, stopping for any length of time was scary. He might have to think. And he didn't want to do that.

Because then he'd have to admit that he'd actually thought that maybe Harris wouldn't have minded his secret. He should have known better.

He blinked. How had he missed Harris's car that was parked in his driveway?

Pulling the yellow knob, he set the brakes with a long hiss. A sound he wanted to emulate. It had been five days, and she hadn't called. Now she was parked in his drive. What could she possibly want?

He checked the engine temp before shutting his rig off and climbing out of the cab. Wary.

She appeared around the house, a cute, ruffled green apron tied around her slender waist. Her loose hair tumbled down her shoulders and chest. A long, very librarianish skirt covered most of her legs, and her feet were tucked in serviceable shoes.

He stopped with one hand on the door of his truck, like maybe he'd need to make a quick getaway.

She held his hat up. "I thought you might want this."

He ran a hand through the hair he'd never cut. He hadn't taken the time to buy a new hat this week, but he hadn't figured he'd ever see that one again.

"Thanks," he said.

She walked a little closer. He held his ground. "I thought you might want me to teach you to read." Her face gave nothing away.

He, frankly, was a little surprised. Whatever he'd been expecting from her, it wasn't that. He jerked his head at his truck. "Right after you learn to drive this."

Her eyes widened and moved to his truck. Her lips flattened.

Yeah. That's what he thought. Everyone thought reading was so easy. It wasn't easy to some people.

"I've got a casserole in the oven. You can start to teach me as soon as it's done." She pulled her phone out of her pocket and looked at it. "Although DeShaun is going to be here in fifteen minutes. And Miss Beulah is bringing Pap." Her chin lifted. The tilt of her face made her freckles more prominent.

He searched her face, looking for the vulnerability or the hidden agenda. What was she saying? The hard wall that he'd spent the week trying to build up around his heart, all the time he'd spent trying to convince himself he didn't care what Harris thought, everything, it was all crumbling. He sucked a breath in, trying to be strong.

"You don't really want to learn to drive." He said it flatly, spitting the words out so they didn't choke him.

She walked closer, stopping beside his front fender. Close enough he caught her sassy-serious scent. It toyed with his nose, seducing his good intentions. He tightened his grip on the door pocket.

"No," she said softly, "I don't. Will you hate me if I don't know how?"

He didn't know how he felt, what he wanted—he wanted to run, he wanted to stay—but one thing he did know. "I will never hate you."

She looked down, shifting her feet. "Now that you've brought the subject up. I was kind of wondering how you really do feel..." She looked him in the eye. "About me."

He didn't say anything.

"I mean, I think I kind of know. And, maybe since you've done so much for me, maybe I should go first?"

"Shoot," he said, not sure if he wanted to know. But he wasn't the kind to run. Except that's exactly what he'd done this week, since he walked out of practice Saturday night. Run.

"I've been here every day this week. In your house. Because the door isn't locked. I've waited for you to come home. I've called your brothers and forced my friends to keep tabs on their husbands and let me know if they could figure out what you were doing. That's how I'm here now, by the way. Cassidy called and said that you'd dropped your trailer."

She paused, putting her hand on his fender, touching lightly along the edge. "I didn't leave any notes, and I didn't text you. I figured I'd just wait." She clasped her hands together and faced him square on. "I love you. I've missed you. I'm sorry I didn't get my mouth working before you walked out Saturday night. Maybe I should have run after you, but you'd shocked me. Twice, and it took me a few minutes to recover."

He dropped his hand from the door and took a step toward her, covering her hand with his over the fender.

"I wasn't lying Saturday night. It wasn't a joke. I can see how you might misunderstand."

"I know you don't lie. I knew you were serious. I wasn't expecting you to quit."

"I wasn't expecting Ransom to show up."

She grunted. "Me either."

"I wanted to make the decision easier for you." That was the honest truth. He had seen the conflict in her eyes and had gone with his knee-jerk reaction to solve it.

Her lips pursed. "You took away my right to make the decision."

He shrugged, unimpressed. "You can thank me. I handled it so you didn't have to choose between the man that you seem to enjoy kissing and the man who would do a professional job for your play."

Her eyes narrowed. "There's no 'seeming' to it. And it wouldn't have been a hard decision. I wanted you. I still want you." She closed the distance between them, putting her hand around his waist. His chest pumped in and out.

"I'm here." His voice scratched out.

Harris's lips flattened in annoyance. "I told you how I feel. I'd appreciate it if you would do the same for me."

He swallowed. "It hasn't changed. Not since high school."

"When you dumped the paint on me?" She lifted a brow, all hints of irritation gone.

"Are you ever going to let that go?"

She leaned back, keeping her arms around him, looking into his eyes, and waiting.

He looked deep into her eyes, willing to bare his soul for her. "I love you. I can't even tell you how much."

"Good. Now that's settled..." Her phone buzzed against his leg. She reached in the pocket of her apron and pulled it out. "Hello?"

He ran his hands up her back, wondering how long DeShaun and Miss Beulah and Pap were going to stay. Of course, Harris probably had play practice.

"You're kidding... No... Oh no!... Please, tell me you're kidding. No, you cannot be serious... No, of course. I'll see what I can do... We'd have to give it all back. Somehow...right. I'll call you later. Goodbye." She dropped her phone back into her pocket and leaned her forehead against Turbo's chest.

"What's the problem?" he asked.

"Grace missed practice last night. She was diagnosed with mono this morning. Daddy Warbucks just called her because he's having the same symptoms, and he's headed to the doctor right now, but it's probably mono for him."

"So, couldn't they still power through the play? At least tomorrow?"

"The doctor said bedrest. It takes weeks to get over it. Actually

Daddy Warbucks isn't going to the doctor himself. He was so exhausted his mother had to come and pick him up."

"Wow. I might have been able to step back in for Daddy Warbucks, but I can't play Grace." He'd have to kiss himself. Then an idea popped into his mind, so brilliant that it shocked even him. "But..." He put a finger under her chin. "You could."

Her eyes got wide, her mouth formed an "O," and she shook her head, trying to pull out of his arms.

He held on.

"No. No way. There is no way I'm getting up on that stage and taking on the role of Grace."

"Why not? You have the lines memorized." It seemed reasonable to him.

Her eyes were wide. Wild almost. "I do. But I'm not an actress."

"I'm not an actor."

She blinked. Her body trembled. "I can't even conceive of being in front..."

"You could do it."

"No."

She'd pushed him to open up, to take a bigger risk than he'd ever done before. Maybe she needed to do the same. "So you'd let the whole play get cancelled, you'd return all the money that people have already paid for the tickets, you'd let your dreams of a hospital library go down the drain, just because you're scared to get up in front of people?"

"Yes?"

"I can't let you do that. Gotta say, Rissy, if I can stand up in front of all those people and admit that I can't read...you know, I half expected the school district to call this week and demand my diploma back."

"They can't do that."

"Well, they have to know by now that I paid for it."

His words caused her eyes to flicker. Pain, maybe? "I wondered how you got through. I mean...I know you are an expert at misdirection." She smiled. "I think that's why you're good at magic."

He snorted. "Probably right."

"But tests? Writing assignments? Essay questions."

"They don't give the 'slow' kids essay questions." He could count on one hand the number of times he'd had essay questions.

"You're anything but slow."

"That's the label." It was what it was.

"Not anymore."

"Oh, come on. There have to be other kids like me that can't do the work and figure out how to game the system."

"You're probably right. Just new ways now. Electronic ways, maybe." There were always ways. He'd found them then, and if he were in school today, he'd figure out something. Plenty of other kids could, too.

"Maybe." It didn't matter anymore. "But that's off the subject. I have a deal that you can't resist."

"Hardly."

He paused, for full dramatic effect. "You play Grace, and I'll let you teach me to read."

"You're right. That is hard to resist."

"Thought so." He shrugged. "I can't promise that you'll be successful. After all, I spent four years truly trying to master phonics and reading."

"I wondered if it was an eye coordination or brain wiring problem. Like dyslexia or maybe eye tracking?"

One side of his lip turned down. "Maybe. I don't know."

"There's a lady who uses the library with clients. She does some things that help with brain wiring, which includes dyslexia. I've also seen her doing eye exercises. I think it'd be worth a try. But—" She paused and stared him in the eye. "I don't want you to think in any way that my feelings are contingent on you being able or not being able to read. Is that clear?"

He lifted a shoulder. "Speak for yourself. I don't think I'll love you anymore if you don't play Grace."

She laughed. "That's not fair."

"What's the saying? All's fair..."

"In love and war." She chuckled again. "Not this."

"I want you to do it. I don't want to kiss anyone but you." He lowered his head. "Actually, I think we should start practicing right now."

She lifted her head. "If you insist."

A car motor sliced through the chilly afternoon air. It slowed. Gravel crunched. Turbo groaned. "Maybe that's for the best. When you kiss me, I get a little crazy anyway."

"That's so?"

"Plus, we have play practice to do tonight."

"Oh, gosh. I'm not sure I can." Another tremble ran through her.

"I am." He tightened his arms around her before letting go. They turned to meet their guests.

"Is that DeShaun?" Turbo squinted up the street. It looked like DeShaun, but the kid was carrying a... "Is that a baby?"

"Does he have a baby sibling?"

"Not that I know of," Turbo said. "You mind helping Pap and Miss Beulah out? I'll see what's going on with DeShaun."

She nodded, and he jogged across the yard and down the street.

"Yo. Turbo." DeShaun moved his shoulders. "Can't slap your hand, bro. I've got a package."

"That package is a good imitation of a live baby."

"Yeah. My dad kicked my mom out and brought this new chick home. She claims this is his. If that's true, I've got a sister I didn't know about until Tuesday. Where ya been anyway?"

"Working. Some of us do that, you know."

"Shut up. I'm gonna work when I get old enough."

"You better." Turbo smacked him on the head, because he didn't want to bump his shoulder. "Why are you walking around with the baby?"

"They told me to take her."

Turbo looked closer at the wrapped bundle. It didn't look very old. "You have anything to feed it? Wasn't there a stroller that comes with it? Diapers?" Not that he was changing any.

"It's a she. Be respectful," DeShaun said with a sniff.

"Stuff? Does *she* come with stuff?"

"Nope."

"That's it?"

"Yep."

"That's all she came with?"

"Yep."

"Holy frig." Turbo didn't know much about babies, but he did know, from watching his brother's kids, that when they got hungry, they needed to be fed immediately, or things got very loud, very fast.

"I've got it," DeShaun insisted.

"You're, what, fourteen?"

"Yeah."

"Okay. I guess this is legal." He turned, making a mental note to have Harris call Kelly, who was in social work, and talk to her about a small visit to DeShaun's house. No need to mention that to DeShaun. "Come on. Let's eat. Miss Winsted has play practice, and I guess I'm in it again."

"Thought you quit?"

"How'd you hear that?"

"I've been sitting in the back, watching. Wish I could be in it." He shrugged. "I'm gonna be in the next one. Miss Winsted said I could."

"Oh?" He hadn't realized there was going to be a next one, and he hadn't realized DeShaun wanted to be in it.

"Yep."

"Well..." He eyed the baby again. At least it was sleeping now. "Come on. Gotta eat."

DeShaun carried the little bundle close to his chest, and they walked to the house.

Pap took one look, whipped his glasses out of the case in the pocket of his shirt, and looked again. "What do you have there, DeShaun?" He peered a little closer. "Looks like one of them real-life doll things."

"A baby?" Miss Beulah said with a raised brow.

"Yeah. One of those," Pap said with a nod.

Harris peeked at the baby. Turbo's heart melted at the sweet longing on her face. Visions of little red-haired babies running around all over the place filled his active mind.

She looked up, blinking and meeting his eye. The look disappeared as though it never was.

"We'd better get in and eat before that casserole burns." She smiled like she didn't have a care in the world, tucked her arm in Miss Beulah's, and started toward the back door.

Chapter Nineteen

Turbo sat on the pediatric playroom floor with his head bent over a plastic tablecloth. The buzz of the dog clippers rang sharply in his ears. He squeezed a piece of gauze against his right ear where Quincy had accidentally caught the lobe. That was one good thing about cutting his hair in the hospital—plenty of first-aid bandages to stop the bleeding.

Forcing himself not to flinch as the blades hummed slowly by his left ear, Turbo studied the big clumps of hair that had already fallen to the plastic. The feet of several children topped off his line of sight. More kids than he'd expected had come to see him "get bald." He should have but hadn't considered the kinship they would feel with him as his hair slowly fell from his head.

"Okay, let's see that," Quincy said as she snapped the clippers off.

The kids tittered. Quincy held up a mirror. His entire head was bald except for one horizontal section halfway up the side of his head, which stuck out like the lone survivor of a terrible shipwreck.

"We should dye that blue."

He gave the nurse that had spoken a flat-mouthed look. "Daddy Warbucks did not have blue hair. I ought to know. I've seen the movie at least twenty times." At least.

"Well, it'd be funny."

"Hilarious," he deadpanned.

"Leave it there!" a couple of the little boys shouted.

"Next time," Turbo promised. It was high enough that his hat would cover it. And it'd be worth it to see the kids smiling again. They hadn't had this much fun in a long time. If he'd realized that something as simple as him shaving his head would cause so much excitement and laughter, heck, he'd have done it years ago.

"All right. I'm going to finish it off. I even left your ear attached."

"Yeah, I appreciate that. You reshaped my other one. Maybe it won't stick out so far now."

The kids laughed as Quincy snapped the clippers back on. Soon all his hair had fallen to the sheet. Turbo removed the garbage bag from around his neck and helped Quincy put the clippers away.

"I appreciate it."

"Sure. It was fun. Maybe I'll cut hair when I get out of here." She gave a shy smile.

"You'd better cut mine for free, since I'm the one who helped you find your calling," Turbo joked.

"Hey, we need everyone to line up over there, so I can get your picture with Turbo and his bald head."

The kids cheered and laughed and ran over to the brightly painted wall the nurse indicated. Turbo allowed the kids who wanted to touch his head to do so and good-naturedly went over with them.

What would Harris think of his decision? He'd not really spoken with her about it. He'd meant to, but she'd been busy, and while she seemed okay with him, and they'd said "I love you" to each other, he didn't feel like their relationship was back to normal, whatever that was. He didn't want to make it worse, if there was the possibility to make it better.

Too late now. He couldn't glue the hair back on. He smiled for the picture, wishing he'd made sure to talk to Harris first.

After slapping a couple kids high five, thanking Quincy again, and picking up his garbage, he pushed open the double doors and headed out to his truck.

His phone buzzed before he made it to the elevator.

It was a text from a number he recognized as his biggest account. He clicked through the familiar sequence to get his phone to read it.

"We have an emergency load of corn that needs to be delivered in Spring Glen by two o' clock this afternoon. Let me know right away if you can take it."

He closed his eyes and did some figuring. If nothing went wrong, he'd be back with an hour to spare for the dress rehearsal.

If his truck hadn't been down longer than he expected and if this weren't his most important vendor, he wouldn't even consider it. But he couldn't risk it. Too many things could happen, and he wouldn't let Harris down.

He clicked on the texting speaker and spoke a quick sentence telling them to give the load to someone else.

HARRIS PEEKED AROUND THE CURTAIN. She shouldn't. She knew she shouldn't even look, but she couldn't help it. On one hand, she was glad people showed up, on the other, the more people, the more nervous she got. Her insides felt like a chicken on a spit—roasted and slowly turning.

At least looking around the curtain took her mind off her biggest problem. More than remembering her lines, more than making sure everything was ready, more than this being her first public performance, ever, there was one thing that was killing her.

Turbo wasn't here.

All cast members were supposed to be onsite at five. They were supposed to be dressed and ready for their performance by six. The play started at seven. They'd spent some of the last two hours going over various sticky parts. Without Turbo.

Where was he?

He'd been very dependable. He'd taken her seriously. He'd done his best for the play, and after she'd found out that he couldn't read, his performance had been all that much more amazing.

Still... She checked her phone again. Five 'til seven. Her lips pressed together, and her stomach rioted. She put the phone down on the small table where she always kept it during rehearsals. The busyness and rushing behind her reminded her that she needed to be helping put things together.

She turned. Still not sure what, exactly, they'd do if it were time to start and Turbo still hadn't showed up.

Her phone buzzed.

She grabbed it off the small table.

Gonna be late.

Turbo texted? She knew there was a speech-to-text app, but he'd never used it for her. She supposed it was more because of the effort of having the reply read to him. So she didn't answer, even though she wanted to send a barrage of questions. How late? Why? Are you okay? Will you make it in time?

Her phone buzzed again.

Start without me. I'll be there for my entrance.

That didn't exactly reassure her, but it was better than what she had. And it must mean that he was okay?

She had to pull herself together. Surely he had a great excuse, and this wasn't some kind of prank.

Focusing on the other actors, Harris was able to get the play started only five minutes late. Better late than early. It would give Turbo more time to get there, wherever he was.

When it was time for the scenery change to the Warbucks mansion, she waited backstage with Camila, looking around, hoping to catch a glimpse of Turbo. This was the scene. He should be here. Somewhere.

"Where's Turbo?" Camila whispered to her, for only the third time all evening. A fact for which Harris was grateful.

"He was running late. He said he'd be here." She hoped her smile was reassuring, even though her face felt like hard wax.

Camila pressed her lips together.

"You're doing great," Harris whispered in her ear.

The scenery was set, and the stagehands jogged off. A hand gripped her shoulder.

"You hate me?" Turbo whispered in her ear.

She jerked around. Taking him in, breathing a cool sigh of relief, even as her brain noted something was out of place.

"Your hair?"

Turbo's mouth moved up in a slow grin. "Quincy cut it. Gave me an idea."

"One of your crazy ideas made you late?"

Camila grabbed Sandy and walked out onstage.

"It was the best one I ever had." He grabbed her arm, pulling her to him and pressing his lips on hers. "I love you. Break a leg."

She didn't quite get her big grin schooled into the appropriate expression before she walked out onstage.

The rest of the play went by in a blur. She had no trouble giving Turbo heated glances. The chemistry between them almost crackled. He stumbled over his lines during the car scene, and she missed a couple of notes in the song at the end.

Turbo had never kissed Mia during practice, although Ransom and Mia had shared a sweet, closed-mouth smooch when they practiced together. He surprised her when he kissed her full on the lips at the end.

She still hadn't recovered from the kiss when Cassidy walked out onstage before the curtain closed.

Turbo held Camila's hand on one side and Harris's on the other. He squeezed her hand. "Listen."

Cassidy held a mic. "I hope everyone enjoyed the show. Tomorrow is the first actual scheduled performance. However, I want to say, before you leave, that Turbo Baxter, who played Daddy Warbucks tonight, pulled an actual Daddy Warbucks today."

She paused to let her words sink in. "He had been called to work, but instead of going, he went around to the doctors at the pediatric cancer unit—where the money from this play is going to fund books for a library—and asked for the kids in the unit to be allowed to come."

People started clapping, and Cassidy waited for them to stop before she continued. "Of course, it's highly irregular. The kids are susceptible to germs, and many of them are hooked to monitors constantly. It is absolutely unheard of for these children to be able to leave. But Turbo has a way of figuring things out, and although some of the sickest children were not able to be here in body, we've been livestreaming the performance to them."

She moved the mic to the other hand and turned to the side a little. "Turbo rented a bus and brought the rest of the children over, along with several doctors and nurses and parents. They're going to hop up onstage for a minute and say 'hi,' then Turbo needs to get them back to the hospital. But we wanted you to see why they've done all this work. Every penny of every ticket goes toward the library for these kids. Come on up, guys."

Cassidy moved her arm in a "come here" gesture, and about fifteen kids, monitors and IV lines trailing behind, as doctors and nurses helped them along, moved up and across the stage. Most of them were just as bald as Turbo, and all had huge grins on their faces.

Turbo leaned down beside Harris. "That's why I was late."

"What am I going to do with you?" she asked with a shake of her head.

"Marry me," he replied.

She gasped. "Is this another of your pranks?"

"The timing's all wrong, I'm doing it badly as usual, but I'm dead serious. Would you marry me?"

She didn't have to think about it twice. "Yes."

He grinned, but there was still a cloud behind his laughing eyes.

"What?"

He looked out at the line of kids. The audience was on its feet, and the applause shook the rafters in the old theater. "I was going to bring DeShaun, too. But the police were there to arrest his father and the woman who just moved in for armed robbery. Social services was there taking the kids. It was a mess. I left, but..."

"We'll go see. Actually Cassidy might be able to help us. Or Kelly."

"I wondered if we might be able to move our marriage up and become foster parents pretty fast or..." He paused, studying her face. "Or adoptive parents."

"Let's try." She could hardly believe it. It wasn't very long ago that she thought about everything she did for days or longer, and here she was making two life-changing decisions on the spur of the moment. But nothing had ever felt more right.

Harris squeezed Turbo's hand. "After all, DeShaun is kind of the one who started this all."

Epilogue

Five months later

Turbo balanced a bottle in one hand and his soon-to-be daughter in the other arm. Kerrigan. That's what they'd named her. Not that he could barely remember his own name when she smiled up at him like she was doing now.

"You two are just staring at each other. Doesn't she want her bottle?" Harris walked over and slipped an arm around him.

Turbo turned his head and placed a kiss on her cheek. "Thought you and DeShaun were making cookies for me?"

"We did. I came to get the baby so you could eat with both hands."

Turbo stared at his wife. "You're making fun of me."

She took the bottle from him. "I was making a joke. You said you like it when I laugh. Well, I like it when you laugh, too."

She couldn't have said that better. One of his favorite sounds in the world was his wife laughing. He handed the baby to Harris, kissing his wife sweetly before straightening and looking out over the backyard. "This warm weather probably isn't going to last."

"No. We'll have more cold weather before things warm up for good."

"And I'll be out of school for the year."

"Is it that bad?"

"I look forward to it. I get your undivided attention."

She balanced the baby in one arm, holding the bottle with the same hand, and handed him a letter he hadn't seen she had.

"I think you can read this for yourself."

Turbo gave her a look. He would live with his attention deficit disorder for the rest of his life, but eye tracking exercises and a few other magic tricks, as he called the brain exercises Harris had researched for him, had put his learning to read on the fast track. He still wasn't confident, and when he hadn't slept for a while, his eyes would jump all over the page, but he'd made huge progress in the last few months. He'd spent most of his spare time over the winter working on it, though. He didn't want Harris to ever be embarrassed of her husband, although she insisted it wasn't possible.

He looked the envelope over. An official state address was in the upper left corner. His lips slowly turned up, even before he opened the envelope.

He read, taking a little extra time because a few of the words were long and unfamiliar, but his smile never dimmed. It got bigger.

"This means they're ours." He said it as a statement, but he lifted his brows at her, still wanting her to confirm that DeShaun and Kerrigan were, indeed, officially adopted.

"It's unprecedented how fast it happened."

"That's what happens when a man has a wife with lawyers and social workers as friends."

"You know, not to change the subject or anything, but you never mentioned your older brother."

"Torque and Tough. You know them both." He was being deliberately dense, because he didn't really want to talk about...

"There's another brother."

"I don't know anything about him."

"His name?"

"That's a sore spot." Somehow the older brother who had left as their mother died of cancer had been the only one in the family who had gotten a decent name.

"Ben." Harris handed him the bottle with a lifted brow. "His name is Ben."

"I guess so."

"I think we ought to look him up."

"No. After knowing how my dad was. And after he left just when the family really needed him, I'm not interested."

"He's your brother."

Turbo's phone buzzed in his pocket. He gave Harris the darkest look he could muster before answering. "Torque. What's up?"

"Gram's in the hospital. You probably ought to come. Mercy Hospital."

"We'll be there." He swiped the phone off. "Gram's in the hospital."

"What happened?"

Turbo paused as he gathered the baby's blanket and carrier. "Don't know. Didn't think to ask."

Her eyebrows stayed pinched in concern, but she shook her head with a smile on her face. "I can call Quincy and see if she's available to keep an eye on the kids."

Turbo followed Harris inside, greeted by the smell of fresh-baked cookies. "Has she heard about the publisher?"

Harris turned to smile with real pride. "She's going to self-publish it. She and Elsie are going to go together. They've already raised money by selling cookies and babysitting. Anything they make after costs is going toward the library."

"There's not too much the hospital library needs. Your play outfitted it with a ton of books and a bunch of iPads."

"No. They've adopted a library in Mexico. I thought I told you they were taking a trip down to Guadalajara in the spring."

"Sounds dangerous."

"No more dangerous than cancer."

He pulled her toward him, Kerrigan and all. "Maybe it was your cancer that gave you the courage to take a chance on me."

She smiled.

"And I'm happy with black-haired, black-eyed babies with chubby cheeks and sparkling grins." He shrugged. "Red hair is overrated."

"Well." Harris bit her lip. "I've been meaning to talk to you about that."

"You want to dye your hair?" He couldn't stop the alarm that ran through his chest. Of course he'd still love her if her hair were blue, but...could one dye red hair blue? She'd made him watch *Anne of Green Gables*, on their wedding night if he wasn't mistaken, and Anne's attempts at dyeing her red hair had not turned out well. He'd have to think of how to console Harris when her hair turned green.

"No." She patted Kerrigan's back. Kerrigan let out a polite little burp. "Actually, I'm pregnant."

"Holy frig." He was worried about Gram and wanted to get to the hospital as soon as possible. But... "Are you sure?"

"I didn't believe it myself until I made an appointment. The doctor did an ultrasound right there in the office. Her heart is beating."

"Her?"

"I'm not sure I can handle a miniature Turbo hurricane."

He laughed. "I'll help."

"I'm counting on it."

DeShaun stepped out from the kitchen, an apron tied around his thin waist, a cookie in each hand.

Turbo waved the envelope. "This says you and Kerrigan are officially ours."

"Really? Awesome, dude." He gave a shy grin. "I mean, Dad."

Right there, Turbo's heart burst. As long as Gram was okay, there was no possible way he could be any happier.

[Join Jessie's list and be the first to know about new releases and sales on her books!](#)

Read Second Chance with You, the next book in the Baxter Boys series where the mysterious Ben Baxter gets his book! He's back in Brickley Springs, faking a marriage and trying not to fall for his boss. Keep reading for a sneak peek now.

Sneak Peek of Second Chance With You

Riley Coleman's phone buzzed. She kept her hands folded in her lap and didn't move.

"That terminal is sitting at the confluence of the turnpike, I80 and I99, right in the middle of central Pennsylvania. We're perfectly positioned to be everywhere and go anywhere." Her dad's booming voice filled the corner office of Coleman Trucking, Inc. in Rutlege, Maine.

Her phone stopped buzzing. Riley didn't twitch.

"It should be our top performing shop. It should be number one in the country. We have state-of-the art computer systems and mechanics from the top schools anywhere." His face brightened like the red of her mother's old counter tops. "But it's not. It's the worst performing diesel garage we own. The bottom in just about every measurable area."

He stood, tall, as always, with a slightly larger waistline than when Riley had last seen him at Christmastime. "It's not just because you're my daughter. It's because you've made this shop, in Nowheretown, Maine, the best-performing shop in the country. The job in Pennsylvania is yours by rights."

Riley rose as well. Only his old office desk, ponderous and glowering, stood between them. "I can do the job." Her voice sounded capable and bold. A direct contrast to the timorous skittering of her heart.

"Bold as brass. That's what you've always been." Her dad smiled, a pleased I'm-proud-of-my-daughter smile. The kind she lived for.

She gave him a cool, confident smile in return. The smile she'd perfected over the years of demanding confrontations when her father insisted on and expected almost super-human effort from her. But everything she'd worked for was almost within reach: make the shop in Pennsylvania successful, get the corner office, see her dad's approval.

"I need you down in Brickly Springs by the end of next week."

"I'll be there," she said, her confident tone covering her chaotic thoughts. Less than seven days to wrap things up at the shop in Maine, move out of her apartment and find somewhere to live. *No problem, Dad.*

He nodded, pacing behind his desk. His boots made a soft clomp on the tile floor. Outside the large windows, the late Maine spring was just turning the grass at the edge of the big truck parking area a happy shade of green. A direct contrast to the dark paneling and neutral colors of what used to be his office. Until ten years ago when he expanded his company and moved with his family to Pennsylvania. Riley had come back to Maine six years ago, fresh out of college. She'd worked her way up quickly and had become the manager four years ago.

The same time Ben Baxter had been made shop foreman.

Riley's control slipped and she pulled both lips between her teeth before she forced the tension out of her body and smoothed the features of her face. She wasn't going to think about Ben Baxter.

Except, if she wanted the shop in Pennsylvania to be successful, she didn't have a choice. Not only would she have to think about him, she'd have to convince him to move to Brickley Springs.

Ben Baxter set the last injector carefully on the plyboard and sawhorse make-shift table. He pulled the blue rag out of the back of his pocket and started wiping his hands, looking around at the almost deserted shop.

"Hey, boss. I'm leaving." Fred Tomlin, his gray hair sticking out from under his ball cap in wispy strands, stopped beside the gutted Peterbilt Ben had been working on.

"Thanks for staying and giving me a hand with that core," Ben said. He shoved the rag back in his pocket.

"You still have a meeting with the fancy lady?" Fred asked with a smirk.

Riley Coleman wasn't hated around the shop. She was a fair manager and nice to look at, but with her business suits and perfectly shiny hair and nails, she would never be on their level. Which made her an outsider. Ben never bothered defending her. Not after what she'd done to him.

"Yep." Ben wiped the last of his wrenches off and set it back neatly in the drawer with the rest of the set. "She should be here any minute."

Fred paused in the act of raising his hat and rubbing his mostly bald head. "She's coming here?" he asked incredulously, hooking a finger in the pocket of his jeans. Most shops had a uniform policy. Ben had done away with it first thing when he'd become foreman. That wasn't the only change he made, but by the time the higher-ups had realized what was going on, they couldn't argue with his improved output numbers. *Riley* couldn't argue. This wasn't their first meeting.

"Said she was." Ben carefully wiped off his three-quarter inch socket.

This was their first meeting, however, in the shop. Every other time he'd been called on the carpet, he'd had to stand like a bad little schoolboy hanging his head in front of the principal's office. Never again. His sisters had graduated from high school and had several years of additional training under their belts. He could finally afford to take the risk he'd always wanted to take.

Fred's eyes swept over him, taking in the grease on his tee shirt, arms and face. It mixed with the blood he'd wiped there when his forearm had clipped a jagged piece of metal after cutting off a stubborn bolt.

"Ain't you gonna clean up at all?"

"Nope." He gave Fred a grin. "Won't hurt the woman to see what a working man looks like."

Fred returned his grin and shrugged before turning. "See ya tomorrow."

"Flip the lights out for bays one and two before you go."

Fred didn't answer, just hit the switches on the way out the door.

Maybe he should have cleaned up, at least washed his hands and arms. But, with his sisters raised, he had a hard time caring about impressing the snotty daughter of the owner of one of the biggest trucking companies in the country.

Riley could come to him. He didn't give a flip, because he was quitting.

Sign up for Jessie's newsletter! Get a free book, access to exclusive bonus content, get fun and funny updates on her life on the farm and more!

Read More Jessie!

Tap here to see all of Jessie's books!

A Gift from Jessie

View this code through your smart phone camera to be taken to a page where you can download a FREE ebook when you sign up to get updates from Jessie Gussman! Find out why people say, "Jessie's is the only newsletter I open and read" and "You make my day brighter. Love, love, love reading your newsletters. I don't know where you find time to write books. You are so busy living life. A true blessing." and "I know from now on that I can't be drinking my morning coffee while reading your newsletter – I laughed so hard I sprayed it out all over the table!"

Claim your free book from Jessie!

Escape to more faith-filled romance series by Jessie Gussman!

The Complete Sweet Water, North Dakota Reading Order:

Series One: Sweet Water Ranch Western Cowboy Romance (11 book series)

Series Two: Coming Home to North Dakota (12 book series)

Series Three: Flyboys of Sweet Briar Ranch in North Dakota (13 book series)

Series Four: Sweet View Ranch Western Cowboy Romance (10 book series)

Spinoffs and More! Additional Series You'll Love:

Jessie's First Series: Sweet Haven Farm (4 book series)

Small-Town Romance: The Baxter Boys (5 book series)

Bad-Boy Sweet Romance: Richmond Rebels Sweet Romance (3 book series)

Sweet Water Spinoff: Cowboy Crossing (9 book series)

Small Town Romantic Comedy: Good Grief, Idaho (5 book series)

True Stories from Jessie's Farm: Stories from Jessie Gussman's Newsletter (3 book series)

Reader-Favorite! Sweet Beach Romance: Blueberry Beach (8 book series)

Blueberry Beach Spinoff: Strawberry Sands (10 book series)

From Strawberry Sands to: Raspberry Ridge (12 book series)

Swoonfully Jolly Holiday Stories:

Holiday Romance: Cowboy Mountain Christmas (6 book series)

Cowboy Mountain Christmas Spinoff: A Heartland Cowboy Christmas (9 book series)

New and Much Loved: Mistletoe Meadows (4 books and counting!)

Laughing Through the Snow: Christmas Tree, PA Sweet Romcoms (6 short reads)